"Come On, Tod, Let's Go for a Swim Like We Did Yesterday."

Tod didn't need asking twice, and soon the pair of them were swimming from rock to rock, leapfrogging and swiping at each other, completely unaware that the current was getting faster and faster.

"Tod!" called out Copper, looking around for his friend.

"T-o-d! Come on, stop hiding; I bet you can't reach that pile of twigs before me."

But Tod was nowhere to be seen.

"H-e-l-p. . . ."

Suddenly Copper thought he heard a muffled cry.

"C-C-Cop——"

Copper reached a boulder sticking out of the water and heaved himself up onto it by his front paws. Looking downstream, he felt his heart miss a beat as he saw a dark, furry shape being tossed and turned helplessly in a little whirlpool. He just knew that it was Tod. Somehow he had to try to save him.

Walt Disney Productions'

The Fox
and the
Hound

Based on the Book by
Daniel P. Mannix

Novelization by Heather Simon

AN ARCHWAY PAPERBACK
Published by POCKET BOOKS • NEW YORK

An Archway Paperback published by
POCKET BOOKS, a Simon & Schuster division of
GULF & WESTERN CORPORATION
1230 Avenue of the Americas, New York, N.Y. 10020

Published by arrangement with Walt Disney Productions

ISBN: 0-671-44291-0

First Archway Paperback printing December, 1981

10 9 8 7 6 5 4 3 2 1

AN ARCHWAY PAPERBACK and colophon are
trademarks of Simon & Schuster.

Printed in the U.S.A.

IL 3+

The Fox
and the
Hound

Chapter 1

It was early morning and the sun was struggling hard to break through the misty country air. Everything was silent as all the creatures of the night had gone home to sleep and all the creatures of the day had not yet woken up.

Suddenly the peacefulness was shattered by the excited sound of some dogs howling in the distance; something or somebody was being chased through the forest.

In a sun dappled, dewy clearing the shape of an animal appeared, carrying something in its mouth. It was a mother fox, her sides heaving as she fought for breath, for she had been running for miles trying to save the life of her cub and herself.

After glancing quickly this way and that, the mother fox set her cub down on the ground and allowed herself a few seconds precious rest. But the baying of the dogs grew dangerously nearer all the time. She had to go on.

Picking the cub up by the scruff of its neck, the mother fox ran blindly from the clearing. On and on through the undergrowth she ran, jumping over fallen branches, ignoring thorny bushes that scratched and tore at her glistening red coat.

Eventually she emerged from the forest and followed the course of a small river that wound downward toward some farm buildings. The dogs were getting closer now, soon they too would be clear of the trees. She had to find somewhere to hide.

High up in a tree a large, sleepy looking owl emerged from her hole to see what all the fuss was about and quickly spotted the mother fox as she wriggled her way through a gap in one of the farm fences.

The mother fox stopped and looked all around her to make sure she was alone. Satisfied, she gripped the cub hard between her teeth and made her way toward a clump of very tall grass.

Parting the grass carefully with one paw, the fox gently lowered her son down into his hiding place, unseen by anyone except the watchful old owl.

With one last sniff of goodbye, the mother fox turned and raced away down the hill, aware that the dogs were now only minutes away. Soon she disappeared from view altogether, and the owl was just wondering when she intended to come back for her offspring, when a shot rang out, almost making the owl fall off her branch. A couple of seconds later came another shot and something in the fresh morning air of the countryside told the old owl that the mother fox would never be able to return to collect her baby.

Inside his grassy hideaway the cub was shivering and shaking with fear. His mother had never left him alone before, except to hunt for food, and then he had always been in the comforting darkness of his den, not cold and frightened and wet with dew as he was now.

The owl shifted her position on the branch. Clearly something had to be done about the poor little mite concealed down below. But at that precise moment she had no idea exactly what.

Stretching her magnificent wings wide, the owl flew down and landed, as quietly as she could, near the clump of grass. A couple of steps and the owl was able to part the tall grass with her beak, to find two huge, very frightened brown eyes peering out at her.

"You poor little fellow," crooned the owl gently. "It's alright . . . Big Mama's here."

The little fox didn't look a bit comforted. In fact, the sight of the huge old owl holding out one of her wings to him only served to make him tremble even more.

"You know, you're going to need some caring for . . ." said Big Mama thoughtfully, won-

dering what on earth she could do with the little cub. "Now . . . let's see . . . you're going to need a brand new mother . . ."

Big Mama turned and started to walk away from the clump of grass. But by now little cub had decided that this big feathery creature was definitely friendly and so he had better totter off after her.

"Oh no . . . no . . . no. Not me . . . not Big Mama," laughed the owl as she turned and saw him.

Suddenly they were interrupted by the insistent drilling of a nearby woodpecker. The cub started trembling furiously once again but the owl seemed very excited by the noise, as though it had given her an extremely good idea.

Hurriedly, she pushed the little cub back into the grass.

"Now I won't be long. Don't you move, honey. Big Mama's going to be right back," she told him reassuringly, and with that flew off in the direction of the busy woodpecker.

Dinky perched on a branch and watched as his friend, Boomer, tapped away at the tree trunk. When a reasonably sized hole had appeared, Dinky flew down and stared into the hole.

"Good work, Boomer. We'll get him this time!" he squawked excitedly.

The two woodpeckers leaned as far as they could into the hole.

"Ssh! I think he's in there," cried Boomer.

Suddenly both birds found themselves almost shaken off the branch as Big Mama arrived on the scene.

"Whew!" she cried. "Am I glad to have found you boys, I need your help *now*. C'mon, follow me, follow me."

Boomer looked longingly at the hole he had just made in the tree. Just a couple of minutes more and that caterpillar in there would have been his breakfast.

"Let's go, Boomer. Come On!" squawked Dinky, always ready for any new adventure.

So the three birds took off together, leaving a frightened but very relieved caterpillar, whose name was Squeeks, to peer out at them from the hole.

Big Mama took her two friends to where the little fox cub was hiding.

"Just look at that poor little thing," said Boomer sadly, as the cub peeked out between the blades of grass.

"Don't you worry," said Big Mama comfortingly. "Now we're going to find someone to look after you."

Boomer and Dinky looked at each other, thinking hard about where they could find a new mother for the fox.

Suddenly Dinky gave a little jump in the air.

"Hey . . . I think I've got an idea," he cried and motioned Boomer and Big Mama toward him as he started to explain his plan.

The baby fox looked up at the three whispering birds and wished somebody would tell him what was going on.

"Leave it to me . . . leave it to me!" cried Boomer eventually, as he flew off in the direction of the nearby farm and house, and a little while afterward Big Mama and Dinky followed him, whispering excitedly to each other.

In the house toward which Boomer was heading lived an old widow woman with no children to look after and no friends to call. The Widow was often lonely and whenever she felt that way she would go for a walk in the forest and listen to the birds singing and try to catch sight of the little animals that lived there, like squirrels or rabbits, hedgehogs or badgers. The forest could always cheer her up.

When Boomer reached her house he landed right on the doorknob of the Widow's front door. Taking a deep breath, he rapped on the door as hard as he could with his strong beak.

"Who is it?" called out the Widow, who was very surprised to hear anybody knocking at her door.

Boomer decided he'd better knock again and this time gave the door everything he'd got.

The Widow muttered crossly under her breath and threw the door open wide to see who had been hammering so loudly. But nobody was there.

Poor Boomer had been thrown back against

the wall and his beak imbedded in the door. He had not had time to make his getaway.

The Widow looked around suspiciously.

"Hmm . . . I was sure I heard someone knocking," she said to herself. Then her eye was caught by something white and floppy moving in the garden. "Oh dear! My laundry. Stop it . . . stop it at once, you hear!"

But the Widow watched helplessly as Big Mama and Dinky made off carrying her rather large and stately bloomers between them, one leg in each beak.

"Oh, you pesky birds . . ." called out the Widow, not knowing whether to laugh or be angry at the sight of her bloomers making their way toward the nearby field. She decided the only thing for it was to give chase and hope that her neighbor in the farm wasn't watching out of his window.

"Now!" called out Big Mama from between her clenched beak. And suddenly the bloomers were dropped down . . . down onto the ground, landing neatly on top of the clump of grass in which the little cub was hidden.

"Well, I wonder what got into those birds," said the Widow to herself, as she stooped to reclaim her underwear from where it had landed. "Well, bless my soul! Why it's a baby fox!".

The little cub peered out curiously from his clump of grass. He'd never seen such a large animal before in his life and never smelled such a peculiar smell either.

"Hello, little fellow," the large animal said, in a rather friendly way. "I wonder where your mother is . . ."

The cub bent his neck back as far as it would go and gazed up into the Widow's face. Desperately afraid, but determined not to show it, he swatted bravely at the Widow's hand as she bent down to pick him up by the scruff of his neck.

"Oh come on now . . . I'm not going to harm you. My, but you're a game little rascal, aren't you? There now, calm down. I'm afraid I can't just leave you out here all alone. You'll have to come home with me."

Big Mama, Dinky and Boomer watched as the Widow disappeared with the young cub. They were very pleased with their day's work and hoped they would get a chance to see the little fellow again sometime.

Back at the house the Widow searched out a small bottle and made a teat from an old eye-dropper rubber top which she had in the medicine cupboard. She warmed some milk and watched with delight as the cub drank hungrily and thirstily while lying in her arms.

"Oh my, you're such a dear little toddler," whispered the Widow tenderly. "Say . . . that's what I'm going to call you—Tod."

Tod yawned and fell contentedly asleep on the Widow's lap.

"You know what, Tod? I'm not going to be so lonesome anymore," said the Widow, gently stroking his coat.

Outside the living room window the three birds were still preening themselves on the success of their plan when a loud 'bang' made them

turn around. It was the Widow's neighbor returning home in his old farm truck, which was bumping and swaying noisily toward his house.

Amos Slade was humming quietly to himself as he clung precariously on to the steering wheel of the truck. Now and again he would look through the window into the back of the truck and give a self-satisfied grunt at the misshapen sack that was being jolted around in there. There was nothing Amos Slade liked better than hunting and now the contents of that sack were going to help him track and kill even more.

Outside the farm house, an old hound-dog called Chief was roused from his slumbers by the coughing and spluttering of his master's vehicle. He sat up and watched as the truck ground to a stop and Amos Slade got out and started rummaging in the back.

Finally his master turned and, grinning, held up the sack for Chief's inspection.

"I've got a surprise for you, Chief ol' boy," he called out.

Chief managed to give a sleepy wag of the tail and lumbered forward thinking that he'd better show a bit of enthusiasm for this "surprise."

"Now take it easy," said Slade, as Chief sniffed curiously around the sack.

Suddenly the bag seemed to move a little and Chief jumped back in alarm.

Smiling, Amos pushed his arm deep into the sack and withdrew a wriggling, wet-nosed little puppy dog.

"How's this for a hunting dog?" he said to Chief proudly.

Chief sniffed rather haughtily and looked with disdain at the furry bundle being held up for his inspection. Slade lowered the little fellow to the ground and Chief felt a warm, sloppy tongue brush eagerly over his nose as he bent down to give another inspectory sniff.

Chief jumped back again. Nobody licked *his* nose and got away with it, and he was about to issue one of his sternest warnings when Slade seemed to realize that his 'surprise' wasn't going down too well.

"You may as well get used to him, Chief," Slade said, determinedly. "He's for you to look after from now on." And with that Slade turned toward the house leaving Chief wondering what on earth an old hound-dog like him was supposed to do with a whippersnapper of a young pup.

Chief turned to the pup about to deliver a set of rules, which included not licking other people's noses without an invitation, but to his astonishment the young pup had wandered into the darkness of the large barrel which had served as Chief's kennel ever since he could remember. The very nerve of it!

Chief stalked into the barrel himself and was

about to swat the unfortunate pup when he suddenly realized the little fellow was smiling at him. His anger melting, Chief merely pawed the pup, whom Slade had already christened Copper, and settled down as comfortably as he could in the remaining space.

Copper gave one enormous yawn and settled down himself, his head resting trustingly on old Chief's leg. And, though he would never admit it, Chief began to like the idea of another dog around the place; maybe he could show the little fellow a thing or two, like how to chase badgers or rabbits or foxes.

Chapter 2

The next morning Tod the fox cub wandered out of the Widow's house and looked around for something to do. He was still very sad that his mother had not returned and felt he needed to do something to take his mind off things.

"Hey, there's Boomer and Dinky, maybe they want to play," said Tod excitedly, running off in the direction of the two birds.

But Boomer and Dinky had other things on their minds at that moment.

"Is this the tree, Boomer?" asked Dinky, as they came in to land.

Boomer hopped along a branch toward a hollow in the tree trunk and put his head near the bark, listening carefully.

"This is the place . . . this is the place. I never forget a tree," squeaked Boomer gleefully.

"He won't get away this time!" said Dinky

menacingly. "Hold it, Boomer. I think I hear something."

The two birds listened carefully.

"Oh that's him alright, Dinky. Hey, why don't you fly around and look in the other side, then we'll know exactly where the little varmint is."

Dinky flew around to the other side of the tree and pressed one eye very close to a small hole in the tree.

"Would you look at that!" he exclaimed in amazement, for there sat Squeeks the caterpillar, nonchalantly munching on a leaf and now and again picking his teeth with a pine needle.

"Okay, Boomer," Dinky called out. "He's right there. Yoiks! Watch it!"

Dinky watched, open-beaked, as Boomer's own beak broke through into Squeeks' home, tearing away an entire portion of tree trunk and taking Squeeks with it.

Boomer looked around sheepishly, the piece of bark still clinging to his beak.

"There isn't anything in there," he started to complain to Dinky.

But suddenly, only about half an inch from one eye, Boomer saw the familiar furry shape of Squeeks peering at him from over the top of the speared bark.

"Why you . . .!" Boomer shook his beak and pecked angrily at Squeeks who, after a short

fight through mid-air, had landed miraculously
on another part of the tree trunk.

Boomer gave chase and stabbed the trunk
once, twice, three times in an effort to skewer
the unlucky caterpillar. But Squeeks was far
too quick for him, and managed to sneak
through another hole and out into some concealing foliage.

"Hi, fellas! What are you doing?" called out
Tod, who had just arrived beneath the tree.

Dinky looked down, rather annoyed at this
interruption.

"Stay out of this, kid. This doesn't concern
you," he squawked commandingly.

Tod watched as Boomer suddenly caught

sight of Squeeks disappearing down another hole and started to peck furiously at the narrow branch which connected him to the tree.

But once again his enthusiasm got the better of him, and after one gigantic effort, Boomer suddenly found that he had pecked his branch completely free of the tree and he was left sitting in mid-air.

With one beseeching look at Dinky, Boomer took a speedy downward plunge, landing in an undignified heap near Tod's paws.

"What happened to you?" asked Tod concernedly.

"S-s-shucks! I think I've bent my beak,"

moaned Boomer, going cross-eyed as he tried to inspect the damage.

An angry Dinky flew down and strutted over to the pair on the ground; Boomer's beak was his last consideration.

"Now see what you've done!" he exclaimed angrily. "You've cost us our breakfast!"

"I cost us our breakfast! Why, if you had done a bit more yourself . . ."

Tod looked from one angry bird to the other and decided that neither of them looked as though they wanted to play with him today.

So, pretending to chase a nearby butterfly, Tod ran off thinking "Worms for breakfast . . . yechhh!"

Back at the barn, the Widow was busily milking Abigail, the cow, and turned to smile hello as Tod came in to see what was going on.

Whenever it was milking time, Abigail always swished her tail to and fro, helping to keep the flies away from the pure white milk that was spurting down into the bucket beneath her.

Tod decided that this tail looked the best plaything in the barn and decided to take a swat at it. But Abigail was too clever for him and bowled him over with one swish!

"Tod, stop pestering Abigail," said the Widow, as the cow turned around to give the young cub a disgusted glance.

Tod backed off, nursing his pride, and wandered over to have a look at the mother hen surrounded by her little yellow chicks.

He only wanted to look, but the hen had heard too many tales about foxes—even young ones—from her own mother, and she pecked out angrily at him, chasing him away from her young.

The hen created so much commotion that Abigail started to join in too, mooing and swaying from side to side, so that the poor Widow lost her balance completely and fell right off her milking stool.

"Oh mercy!" she cried, as she landed in a heap in the straw.

Tod looked in surprise at the chaos surrounding him and suddenly felt his tail being nipped by the angry hen who considered he was still far too close for comfort.

Tod started to run, the hen at his heels, and didn't even have time to look around as the Widow called out, "Tod . . . stop it! . . . Abigail!"

The cow was really upset by now and was swaying and stomping as hard as she could. A couple of seconds later and one of her back feet lashed out and knocked the milk bucket all over the floor.

"Oh no!" cried the poor Widow, clasping her hands to her breast. "There goes my milk!"

Tod stopped running and looked up at the Widow woman, not altogether sure if he was the cause of her unhappiness or not.

"Easy, girl, easy. Steady, Abigail, steady. There, there," soothed the Widow. She looked over to where Tod was cowering guiltily.

"Tod . . . you come here!" Tod didn't like the sound of her voice at all, and tried to hide behind an old barrel. "You come here, I said!"

Tod came out cautiously, and walked slowly over to the frowning Widow.

She bent down and picked him up by the scruff of his neck.

"Now just look what you've done!" she said crossly, holding him out toward all the spilled milk.

Tod looked at the milk spewing out all over the floor. He hadn't meant to be naughty and felt really sorry that he had caused the Widow so much trouble. He looked around into her face and gave one of her ears a big, apologetic lick.

"Now don't try to butter me up," the Widow said, trying to be stern. But one look into his sorrowful eyes and she couldn't help but laugh. "Oh, Tod . . . I just can't stay angry with you . . . you little imp! Now, run along and play, and try to stay out of mischief."

The Widow placed Tod gently on the floor and pushed him slightly toward the door.

He guessed from the tone of her voice that he was more or less forgiven and, with a little jump of joy, scampered out of the barn and out into the sunlight, where a passing butterfly caught his attention and he gave chase, the hen, the milk and Abigail forgotten completely.

Copper the puppy dog's morning had been far less eventful. His master had sorted out another barrel and placed it beside Chief's and he had been told to 'Stay' until it was time for lunch.

Now 'staying' was all very well for old Chief, who liked nothing better than to sleep as much of the day away as he could. But for Copper the world was a new and exciting place full of lots of interesting things and smells to explore. It was just such a smell that was intriguing him at that moment. A smell which made his nostrils quiver and his tail wag—even though he didn't know what it was.

"Hey, there, Copper. What are you sniffing at?" asked Chief, lazily opening one eye.

Copper sniffed, deep and long, moving his nose from right to left.

"Something I never smelled before, Chief," he said slowly.

"Hmmm . . . let me see," said Chief, taking a good long practiced sniff himself. After a few seconds he relaxed again, that was an easy one!

"Aw, shucks, Copper. The Master's just cooking grits and fatback. You ought to know that smell by now."

Copper shook his head emphatically.

"N-no. That's not what I smell. I don't know, Chief. It's something else."

Chief shook his head and tutted disapprovingly.

"Hey, sonny, you've got a lot to learn about sniffing and smelling. Now, where do you think you're going?"

Copper had got up, still sniffing excitedly. "I've got to find out what that smell is, Chief."

The Chief frowned, the Master wasn't going to like the young pup going off like that. But he was a determined little creature and the old hound didn't rightly know how to stop him once his mind was made up.

Copper ran off toward the nearby fields, and

called back over his shoulder, "I won't get lost, Chief. I can smell my way back."

"Can't tell these young whippersnappers anything," muttered Chief to himself, watching Copper disappear over the edge of the hill.

Copper's nose was working frantically as he made his way across the countryside. He just knew he was on the right trail, although who or what had made that trail he hadn't the faintest idea.

Finally, he came to an old hollow log where the scent was even stronger than before.

Head down, Copper entered the log, still sniffing madly. Sniff, sniff, sniff, the trail drew his quivering nose to the roof of the log where a hole lead out and through which he could see the sky. He put his nose to the hole and suddenly found another nose smelling his from outside the log!

It was Tod, who ran to the end of the opening and called out to this strange nose, "What are you smelling?"

"I'm on the trail of something," the nose called back.

"Trail of what?" asked Tod, leaning over to try and see the owner of the nose.

"I don't know . . . yet," Copper called out.

The young pup followed the scent all along the top of the log until he appeared at the end, where once again the two young animals met, nose to nose.

"Why . . . it's . . . it's you!" Copper exclaimed, and taking a couple of paces backward, he let out a huge, long howl.

Tod jumped a little bit at the strange sound and stared curiously at the pup.

"What did you do that for?" he asked.

Copper kind of smiled, and puffed out his chest with pride.

"We're supposed to do that when we find what we've been tracking," he explained.

Tod nodded, although he didn't really understand what the pup was talking about. They regarded each other for a couple of seconds and then Tod decided it was time for an introduction.

"I'm a fox. My name's Tod," he said chattily. "What's your name?"

Copper bounced out of the log and sniffed Tod, knocking him over playfully.

"I'm Copper and I'm a hound-dog."

"Gosh, I bet you'd be good at playing hide and seek," said Tod hopefully. "Want to try, Copper?"

Copper put his head on one side. "Can I use my nose?"

Tod shrugged. He didn't mind what Copper used, he was simply happy at having found himself a playmate at last.

Tod decided that he would be the first one to go and hide.

"Okay, now go ahead and close your eyes and count," he told Copper.

The young puppy turned to the log and put his paws over his eyes, "One, two, three," he began.

"No, Copper. Peeking's not allowed," Tod said indignantly.

Copper lowered his head again and started to count, "One, two, three, four . . ."

Unseen by the two friends, an owl had alighted on a branch nearby and was watching them intently.

"Well, just look at that . . ." said Big Mama in amazement. "A fox and a hound playing together." She shook her head; never in her long life had she seen such a thing.

Big Mama continued to watch as Copper took his turn at hiding, then Tod again, and then Copper once more. And whenever somebody was "found" there would ensue a playful skirmish with puppy and fox cub rolling over and over together, barking and squeaking in delight at their games.

At first Big Mama was very happy to see that Tod had found himself a friend, but slowly, as she watched, she became sadder and sadder, for she realized that this friendship could only last for a little while and that either time or the ways of the world would separate the playful pair and make their friendship impossible.

Just as she was thinking all of this, a voice broke into her thoughts . . .

"Copper . . . Copper! Come on, boy, you've got to come home. Copper!"

It was Amos Slade, the hunter, who had come to look for his missing puppy.

Copper disentangled himself from Tod and ran a little way toward the voice. He turned and looked back at Tod.

"Gee, Tod, I've got to go home now. See you." And with that he turned and ran as fast as he could, knowing instinctively that his master was going to be very angry.

For the rest of that day Tod thought about his game with Copper and tried to think of a way to get to see him again. It was in the middle of the night that he had a brilliant idea, and, just as dawn was breaking the very next morning, Tod sneaked from his box in the Widow's kitchen, across the fields and over the hill, to the Hunter's house where the two dog barrels rested outside.

Tod crept up to the smallest of the two barrels. He was sure that this one belonged to his friend.

"Copper!" he whispered. But all he heard in reply was the snoring of old Chief. "Copper! Are you in there?"

This time Copper's smiling face peeked out from the front of the barrel.

"Come on, Copper!" called out Tod.

Copper looked worriedly over at the sleeping Chief and then back at Tod. He so wanted to go and play, but what if . . .

Suddenly he decided, and with a little skip

and a jump he was out and past Chief and together the pair of them ran off over the hill.

They played tag, and hide and seek, and rough and tumble, panting and licking each other in their excitement. And when it was time to stop for a rest, Tod turned to Copper and said, "Copper, you're my very best friend."

"And you're mine too, Tod," Copper agreed, smiling.

"And we'll always be friends forever, won't we?" asked Tod.

"Yes, forever," said Copper.

Then, fully recovered, the pair of them rushed off to go swimming, completely forgetting that Copper had to get back home before Amos Slade discovered he was missing.

"Curses! That Copper pup's gone and strayed off again!" exclaimed Slade when he went out to give the dogs their breakfast.

Slade summoned Chief and together they strode off into the fields to search for Copper.

"If that little rascal's going to make a good hunting dog, he's got to learn to obey orders," said Slade, with Chief striding along by his side.

Soon they reached the brow of the hill and Slade stopped to call out; "Copper! Copper! Come back here, boy!"

Copper stopped splashing Tod and looked over his shoulder toward the sound of the voice. He knew he ought to obey, but they were having such a wonderful time and he still owed Tod for the dunking Tod had given him at the beginning.

The young animals continued with their games until the voice of Slade and the scent of Chief got uncomfortably close for Copper's liking.

The pup clambered out of the water and shook himself dry.

"I've got to go home now, Tod."

"Do you really have to? We're having so much fun," said Tod, looking sad.

"I've got to . . . he sounds awful mad," said Copper, looking fearfully back toward his master. "I'll see you tomorrow . . . bye."

"Don't forget!" called out Tod.

Copper promised that he wouldn't and disappeared from sight.

That night Tod could hardly sleep, thinking about all the fun he and Copper had had together early that morning.

Tod decided that having a friend was quite the nicest thing in the world and couldn't imagine just what he'd done before he met Copper.

Tod's memories of his mother were getting fainter and fainter all the time. This was not because he hadn't loved his mother very much; he had. But foxes, even when they are living in the wild, know that they have to fend for themselves and cannot depend on anybody. And so, from the day he was born, Tod had been learning to be independent.

The next morning, just as the dawn was beginning to break, Tod quietly sneaked out of the Widow's house and made his way over to Slade's property.

It was still quite dark and sometimes the shadows from the trees made him jump. But he was determined to see Copper and have as much time together as possible, so he kept on

going and soon reached the little hill which overlooked the farm.

Climbing to the top he looked down and saw Copper's barrel. He made his way very carefully down the slope so as not to wake old Chief, and soon was close enough to call out.

"Copper! Copper! It's me, Tod," he called out.

Copper's sleepy face appeared at the door of the barrel and blinked hard, trying to make out his friend in the misty light of dawn.

"Oh, Tod . . . I . . . er . . . um . . . I was just having a lovely dream," Copper almost slipped back into sleep again.

But Tod went and stood right in front of him and playfully swatted one of his ears.

"Never mind about your dream. Come on, let's go and play in the forest before old Chief and Slade wake up. We'll have lots and lots of time today. I got up specially early."

"Yes, so I noticed," said Copper, getting up and giving an enormous stretch. "Come on then, I'll race you up the hill."

The two of them ran and ran; up the hill and down again and out, into the forest.

After a little rest, Tod decided that they should play tag and raced off to hide behind a huge old oak tree.

Copper gave him a head start but his active nose soon sniffed Tod out and he leaped on him from behind a tree. They proceeded to roll about on the moss and leaves, scratching and nipping each other playfully, until Copper had had enough and ran off, with Tod in hot pursuit.

The forest was getting lighter and lighter all the time, and the pair were getting farther and farther away from home, so involved were they in their game of tag.

Suddenly the sound of running water made them both stop running and look around. Tod realized that he didn't recognize any of their surroundings, and had just started to be a little bit frightened when a silvery light from a nearby clearing made him want to investigate.

Copper had seen the light too, and together the fox and the hound made their way toward the fast running stream which bubbled and played its enticing water music to them.

"Ohhhhh! Isn't it beautiful!" cried Copper. "Come on, Tod, let's go for a swim like we did yesterday."

Tod didn't need asking twice and soon the pair of them were swimming from rock to rock, leapfrogging and swiping at each other, completely unaware that the current was getting faster and faster.

"Tod!" called out Copper, looking around for his friend.

"T-o-d! Come on, stop hiding; I bet you can't reach that pile of twigs before me."

But Tod was nowhere to be seen.

Copper began to get very worried. He could

feel the water dragging him downstream now, and however hard he paddled, it was very difficult to stay in one place.

"H-e-l-p. . . ."

Suddenly Copper thought he heard a muffled cry.

"C-C-Cop——"

Copper reached a boulder sticking out of the water and heaved himself up onto it by his front paws. Looking downstream, he felt his heart miss a beat as he saw a dark, furry shape being tossed and turned helplessly in a little whirlpool. He just knew that it was Tod. Somehow he had to try to save him.

Copper swam to the side of the bank and managed to drag himself out. Not even stopping for breath, which he sorely needed, the pup raced along the bank toward the shape of Tod which was fast disappearing under water.

"Tod!" Copper called out, shouting to be heard above the water. "Hang on! I'm coming!"

And with that the valiant little hound took a running jump into the rushing water and began to paddle toward his friend.

It was very difficult even to see where Tod was, for twigs and green stuff kept getting in Copper's eyes and mouth. But he kept going just the same, and finally reached the thrashing terrified shape that was Tod.

"Copper . . . Cop . . . aah!" Tod tried to

reach onto his friend, but foolishly opened his mouth and swallowed a bellyful of horrible water.

Copper knew that Tod was quite likely to drag both of them under in his panic, so, swimming around, he took the first opportunity to grab the scruff of Tod's neck in his teeth and, ignoring the resulting cries of pain, pushed off toward the shore.

Several times Copper was forced to let go, and then he just snapped until his mouth found a piece of Tod, any piece, he didn't care. Then he would start swimming and splashing again, determined not to give up.

Copper's stubbornness was to pay off, and after what seemed like an age, the two of them reached the riverbank.

Tod was just about able to help get himself out of the water. Then the two of them lay, side by side, panting and gasping for air.

"Oh, Copper," Tod whispered at last. "You . . . you saved my life. How can I ever thank you?"

Copper turned and smiled at his friend.

"Oh shucks! You would have done the same," he said modestly.

The two young animals began to look around them at the very unfamiliar forest.

"Er . . . Copper," said Tod quietly. "Do you know the way home?"

"Why . . . of course . . . it's er . . . that way.

No . . . no . . . it's that way,'' Copper looked
from this side to that, but he finally had to admit
that, like Tod, he didn't know the way home
at all.

The two young animals stood up and shook
the water from their coats as best they could.

"Well . . . which way shall we try first?"
asked Tod, hoping that Copper's sense of smell
would help them out.

Copper looked around carefully and finally
decided, so off the two of them went, each one
wondering what their owners would say when
they eventually returned.

After some time Tod stopped and flopped
down onto the ground.

"It's no use, Copper. I don't remember this
at all. We must be going in the wrong direction," he said sadly.

Copper was about to suggest trying another
route when the sound of wings beating furiously
made both of them look up.

A huge shadow bore down on them from the
trees and landed in a flurry of angry feathers.

"Phew!" puffed Big Mama, unable to speak
before she got her breath back.

"Oh . . . I've been flying all morning trying
to find you naughty pair. Now just where do
you think you're off to? Don't you know that
everybody else is awake and looking for you?"

"Oh, Big Mama," cried Tod. "I'm so glad
to see you. You see, Copper and I were playing

tag, and then we saw this stream and Copper jumped in and saved my life and then we . . ."

Big Mama flapped her wings up and down to stop the young cub's chattering.

"Yes . . . yes . . . yes . . . well, never mind about all that now. Let's just get you back home and you can tell me all about it later." The old owl took off and circled the two animals on the ground. "Come on, follow me. I'll try not to go too fast."

Copper and Tod raced along the ground just as quickly as they could, while trying to keep an eye on Big Mama up above them. Eventually their surroundings became more and more familiar until finally they reached the hill and their respective homes.

Copper was very worried about Slade's reaction at finding him missing so long and as he got closer he began to drag his steps, much to Big Mama's annoyance who kept calling for him to hurry up.

"Well, Copper, I guess you'd better go," said Tod, staring down at the farm below them. "I hope everything's O.K. for you down there."

"Yeah . . . I just can't imagine what he'll do," said Copper nervously.

"Well, whatever it is, just keep on thinking that I'll be down for you again tomorrow and no matter how sad you are I'm sure I'll be able to cheer you up somehow." Tod smiled, and gave his friend a little shove down toward the house.

Copper trotted forward and then turned, smiling.

"See you tomorrow then, Tod. Bye," and with a final brave flourish of the tail he was off to meet his fate.

Tod watched his friend disappear then made for home himself, and neither of the two young animals guessed for one instant that they had played their last game together.

Chapter 3

The next morning Tod sneaked out and over the hill as usual to collect his friend, Copper.

But when he arrived at the house he found that the poor young pup had been firmly bound to a wooden stump, with no way of getting free to go and play.

"Hey, Copper. What happened to you?" asked Tod, concerned.

Copper looked sad and dejected, his ears hanging low and his eyes big and wide.

"My master says that I've got to stay at home, Tod," said Copper, sadly sniffing his friend's now familiar scent.

But Tod was still in the mood for fun, and jumped playfully onto Copper's back.

"Well, we can play around here then," he laughed.

Copper twisted his head around, out of Tod's grip, and looked anxiously toward Chief's barrel.

"Ssh! Not here, Tod. Not with old Chief over there."

Chief was lying in his barrel, with only his large rump protruding from the front, snoring away as usual.

"Is that him making that awful noise?" asked Tod in disgust.

"He keeps me awake at night," nodded Copper.

Tod got up and wandered over to take a look

at the snoozing old hound dog, who seemed to get larger and larger with every step he took.

Copper tried to follow his friend; he was frightened that Tod would get too close.

"Oh, don't go in there, Tod. He can get awful mean. He's *cranky!"* said Copper, getting more and more nervous for Tod's safety.

Tod walked around Chief's rear end and peered into the barrel, trying to see where the huge animal ended. But his curiosity got the better of him, and Copper watched in horror as Tod began to slide in alongside the old dog, his eyes wide in amazement at such a size.

"Gee, is he big!" Tod exclaimed.

Copper had crept over to stand at the end of Chief's barrel, desperately hoping that his friend would stop this foolishness and come out from this particular lion's den.

"Do you know, Copper, his ears aren't as big as yours?" cried Tod excitedly, from the depths of the barrel.

Copper swiveled his eyes heavenward and crossed his paws as best as he could.

"That's not the part you've got to worry about," he whispered into the barrel.

But Tod was far too interested to listen and, reaching over with his paw, pushed down the side of Chief's lower lip to examine the array of gleaming white teeth that were at least twice the size of his own.

"Goodness . . . look at those teeth!"

"That's the part you've got to worry about,"
said Copper, his own teeth almost chattering
now in fear.

Suddenly Chief started to whimper, as though
in the middle of a dream. His front paw began
to pound the ground and he started to mumble,
"I'm gaining on him . . . he won't get away
now!"

Tod watched curiously and didn't even notice when Copper got kicked away from the
front of the kennel by one of Chief's jerking
back legs.

Copper crept painfully back to the hole and
tried again to make Tod see sense.

"He's waking up . . . get out, Tod! Get out!"

By now Tod was full of misplaced confidence
and leaned dangerously on Chief's muzzle, intently observing the old dog's dream.

"No, it's alright, Copper. He's just dream-
ing. I think he's chasing something."

Copper covered his eyes with his paws and
tried not to listen as Chief's mumblings grew
louder and louder.

"Now I've got him cornered . . . why it's a
big old badger . . ."

"Copper, listen, he's chasing a badger,"
laughed Tod.

"Badger . . ." mumbled Chief darkly. "I'll
get him. No! No, it's not a badger . . . it's a
. . . it's a . . ."

By now Chief had moved his position in his

excitement and Tod found himself being pressed up against the back of the barrel by Chief's snout.

"It's a fox!" cried Chief, whose eyes shot wide open and in his surprise he banged his head hard up on the roof.

"Fox!" he cried, not knowing whether to move his arms or his legs to catch the intruder in this confined space.

Copper was so frightened that he could only return to his own barrel and peer around the corner to see what was happening. He watched as Chief's barrel began to rock wildly from side to side, and didn't dare to think what might become of poor little Tod trapped inside.

But Tod didn't intend to hang around to find out. Using his most cunning moves, he sneaked past the giant frame of Chief who was snapping and snarling and trying to control his arms and legs. Copper watched in relief as Tod's figure raced from the barrel and disappeared out of the yard.

"Run, Tod! Run!" he called out, as Chief got himself the right way around and began to follow the little fox. But Chief was tied to his barrel by some rope and although he could just about manage to drag the whole barrel along with him, it meant that Tod got quite a good head start.

In his terror, Tod dashed straight toward

Amos Slade's chicken house, under some wire, and through a small door to where the chickens were all trying to sleep. At the entrance of the fox the chickens began to fly and squawk and make a dreadful noise. But an even bigger shock was in store for them when Chief's huge head and shoulders appeared at the entrance to their coop.

Poor old Chief got his second awful shock of the morning when it seemed that hundreds of petrified chickens began throwing themselves at his head. Quickly, he withdrew from the coop and stood for a moment, shaking the feathers out of his eyes. Looking around he spied Tod going off in another direction and, still dragging his barrel behind him, he gave chase, this time going around the chicken house and not noticing at all that his kennel was now full of chickens!

Amos Slade threw back his shutters and stared in horror at the scene which met his eyes. He disappeared from view and reappeared at the door, struggling to pull up his pants which he'd pulled on over his snazzy cactus yellow pajama suit.

In one hand he carried his gun, and without bothering to take a very careful aim, began to fire wildly at Tod's retreating form.

Tod began to zig-zag, not knowing which way was home, and found himself almost face to face with Chief and his barrel full of chickens. Turning again Tod raced off in the other direction and Chief turned too, managing to trip up Amos Slade who by now had reached the scene.

High up on a branch Boomer and Dinky clutched each other in terror at the scene below them and with one mind took off and headed for a nearby mailbox hoping for some kind of refuge.

Old Chief was getting further and further behind the young fox, and just as Boomer and Dinky disappeared into the mailbox, Tod saw the very same box and jumped up into it, hoping to hide.

But Amos Slade had seen Tod's tail disappear, and he began firing wildly at the box, which soon began to look like a piece of gruyère cheese, it had so many holes.

Tod leaped from the box, which seemed to explode with departing birds and letters. He wasn't sure but he thought he had a whiff of the scent of home and, with one quick glance behind, made off in the direction from which it came.

Tod raced and raced. He'd gone so far that he had to cross a major road, narrowly missing two passing cars in his desperation to get across. Down a slight hill and Tod came to a small pond which he knew he had to cross. Leaping nimbly onto a rock, Tod made a gigantic effort and managed to make the shore on the other side.

Chief and the barrel had also reached the pond, but the old hound dog was not renowned for his intelligence and although he was able to leap the pond completely, his barrel was not, and just as he landed on the opposite bank his barrel hit the water with a terrific splash, quickly filling up and drawing Chief backward through the air.

Tod took one look back and almost felt a little bit sorry to see the old dog dragged back into the watery kennel, from which he soon appeared, heaving and panting, his cheeks filled with water and his coat absolutely drenched.

Chief looked up and snarled angrily as he caught Tod watching him, but then the sound of a motor engine starting up made them both look around.

It was the Widow, about to go into town to deliver the milk to the dairy, and Tod knew that he had to make one last effort to reach her before he would be safe.

Running as hard as he could, Tod turned the corner of the yard just as the Widow was pulling away from the front of the barn. "Keep running, keep running," he said to himself as he chased the truck down the lane. But it was no good, the Widow was going far too fast.

Then Tod had an idea. She had to go under a bridge, and if he could just reach the bridge first by traveling across country, then he could leap down into the back of the truck and be safe.

Harder and harder he ran, until he could hear the blood singing in his ears. And soon the bridge was in sight.

Tod jumped up onto the balustrade and waited, listening to the sound of the approaching vehicle. There it was . . . now he just had to wait for the right moment and . . . JUMP!

Tod landed in the middle of some of the milk churns and just as he hit the floor of the truck a gun shot rang out, hitting the balustrade on which he had been standing.

Some stones and brick dust clattered down

onto the truck making the Widow turn around in alarm.

"Tod!" she cried, as the worried little face of the fox cub appeared in the back window of the truck and, guessing that Tod had probably been into more mischief, the Widow decided the best thing to do was to step on the accelerator and get both of them out of there as quickly as possible.

By this time Amos Slade too was mobile. He was putting his foot down too and was pelting along the country lanes in pursuit of the Widow and Tod. Suddenly they came into view. Slade hung perilously onto the steering wheel with one hand and tried to take aim at the fox with the other. The muzzle of the gun went this way and that as the old truck bumped along. But Slade was far too angry to give up now, and despite the wavering of the gun he pulled the trigger as hard as he could.

Bang!

One of the Widow's milk churns was the unlucky recipient of the shot and bubbly white liquid began spurting out, leaving a frothy trail for Slade to follow.

Tod peered gingerly out between the churns and nearly slipped on all the milk as the Widow swerved wildly from left to right trying to avoid the shots which Slade kept on and on delivering.

The Widow was really angry and decided that

the only way to get out of this mess was to tell that fool Amos Slade exactly what she thought of his ridiculous behavior.

Without warning, the Widow braked hard and came to a stop. Slade tried to stop too, but skidded on the milk which was still spewing out all over the road.

Tod decided he'd better sit tight, and watched nervously as the Widow climbed down from the driving seat and waited, arms akimbo, for Slade's vehicle to finish skidding.

Just as the truck came to a halt, Chief appeared on the scene, still dragging his barrel behind him and panting hard.

The Widow marched over to where Slade was recovering from his fright.

"Amos Slade! You trigger-happy lunatic! Give me that gun!"

Slade cringed in his seat and was too shocked to give any resistance at all as the Widow reached through the window and grabbed the offending weapon from out of his shaking hands.

Swinging around, the Widow stomped to the front of Slade's truck, brandishing the gun, and took up a firing position.

Amos Slade was shaking even more by now, thinking that the Widow actually meant to shoot him. He covered his eyes and started muttering under his breath.

A shot rang out and Slade jumped about a foot in the air. When he hit his seat again he pinched himself. Yes . . . he was definitely still alive. So what had the Widow done?

From the front of Slade's truck a great gush of steam was shooting up into the sky and boiling water was pouring from the great hole in the radiator made by the Widow's shot.

"My radiator!" screeched Slade, leaping down into the road. "Why you blasted female! I'll . . . I'll . . ."

"Now hold it right there!" barked the Widow, pointing the gun in Slade's direction.

"Watch it! That thing's loaded," he told her, gulping down his words.

The Widow turned the gun around and emptied all the unspent cartridges down onto the ground.

"Well, now it ain't loaded!" she smiled, tossing the empty gun back to Slade so that it hit him hard in the stomach.

"Ooof!" he gasped, cringing. "You pesky woman! Your thieving fox was after my chickens!"

"Rubbish and poppycock! I don't believe it. He wouldn't hurt a thing," said the Widow, glancing down to see Tod hiding between her legs.

"You calling me a liar?" barked Slade. "Why, I saw it happen."

"Amos Slade, that temper of yours is going to get you into trouble one of these days," remonstrated the Widow, brandishing a finger at the red-faced Slade.

"Woman, you ain't even seen my temper yet!" spluttered Slade, who had torn off his hat and was jumping up and down on it on the ground. "But if I ever catch that sneaky fox on my property again I'll . . . I'll blast him! And next time I won't miss!"

The Widow regarded him coolly, like a naughty child, and gathering Tod in her arms turned and left Slade to repair his temper and his radiator.

Chapter 4

The following days Tod found himself a prisoner in the Widow's house. She was so frightened that Slade would hurt the little fellow that she didn't dare let him out for fear of him getting into mischief.

"Oh, poor little tyke," said the Widow, watching Tod gazing so sadly out of the kitchen window. "It's such a shame I have to keep him cooped up."

Tod turned to her and looked beseechingly into her eyes and then out again at the world which beckoned him.

"Oh Tod, stop looking at me like that. It's not my fault, you know. You caused a lot of trouble over at Amos Slade's and if you . . ."

Suddenly a dog barking made both of them turn toward the window.

"Oh, now what are they up to?" said the Widow as she and Tod peered over toward the Slade farm. "Huh . . . it looks like Amos is going on a hunting trip. A long one from the looks of things. Well, good riddance, that's what I say." And the Widow turned back to her chores, leaving Tod to watch the comings and goings at the farm.

Slade was loading his truck with all manner of parcels and packages and cases, while Chief was barking and bouncing around his feet. Copper was nowhere to be seen, but then Tod heard a familiar howl which made him long to see his friend one more time before he was taken away.

Glancing around, Tod noticed that the Widow was totally preoccupied at the stove and, feeling guilty about disobeying her, Tod crept up to a slightly open window and pushed it with his snout. It gave just enough for a small fox cub to squeeze through and without further delay Tod wriggled out and jumped down from the sill, then ran as fast as his legs would carry him toward the Slade farm.

"Blow it! That meddling female really shot up my radiator . . ." moaned Slade, cranking the truck with an old starting handle. Suddenly the engine coughed itself into life. "Well, that's more like . . . keep running old girl."

Copper gave a happy bark. Chief had told him all about hunting trips and they sounded like they could be a whole lot of fun.

"Well, Copper, me and ol' Chief are going to teach you all about hunting," said Slade, bending down to untie the rope which held the pup. "And it's about time too."

Copper cavorted around his legs.

"Atta boy. You're really going to like tracking down those varmints for me," said Slade, rubbing Copper's ears affectionately.

Chief was already installed in the front seat of the truck and Copper bounded up onto the running board and plonked himself down next to the old hound dog.

Chief leaned against the young pup and motioned to the back seat with his head.

"Hey you, get in the back. You've got to earn your right to sit up front, half pint!"

Copper looked confused, but he didn't really mind where he sat and obediently clambered into the back with all the camping equipment, and made himself comfortable.

"Well, boys, we're getting out of here until next spring," said Slade, taking one last look around before jumping into the driving seat.

With a great roar of protest the truck lumbered forward, sending Copper sprawling toward the tailgate of the truck.

The pup poked his head over the end, holding on with one paw, and just as he did so his friend Tod raced around the corner and stopped short at the empty barrels.

In all the excitement Copper had almost forgotten about Tod, but now an enormous wave of sadness washed over him as he realized that they wouldn't see each other for months and months, and he let out the saddest loneliest howl he'd ever given in his life.

Tod watched the truck as it disappeared into the distance. Whatever would he do now that Copper had gone?

"Tod, honey, what are you doing over here?"

Tod looked up as Big Mama flew in and landed on the top of Copper's old barrel.

"Oh, Big Mama, I just wanted to say goodbye to Copper, but I was too late," he said sadly.

"What did you plan to do if you ran into Old Chief?" asked the owl, who had seen the little cub running toward the farm and been very worried for his safety.

"Aw . . . Chief . . ." Tod scoffed. "I can outfox that dumb old dog any time."

Big Mama flapped her wings crossly, and flew down to give Tod a piece of her mind. *Somebody* had to watch out for the silly cub's head.

"Didn't you learn anything a few days ago? Now you listen to me, young fox, because it's either education or elimination."

Tod stared wide-eyed at the angry old owl; she could be as frightening as Chief when she wanted to, but at least she was his friend.

Big Mama went on to tell Tod about all the hunting trips that Chief had been out on and how he was regarded as one of the best hunting dogs in the whole county. What's more, said Big Mama, Chief had the hunter on his side and the hunter had a gun and nobody, but nobody, could argue with a gun and get away with it. Tod looked suitably admonished and kind of agreed with the things Big Mama had been telling him. But then she started to talk about Copper and their friendship and Tod just couldn't believe his ears.

"You see, Tod, Copper is a hound too, just like Chief. And when he comes back from that hunting trip he's not going to be a puppy any more."

"Oh, Big Mama, I know that Copper would never track me down. Why . . . he's my best friend," said Tod, who couldn't believe that Copper would ever knowingly hurt him.

"Ha! Your best friend! You must realize, Tod, that's all past now. Copper will hunt whatever Amos Slade tells him to hunt, and that includes little foxes like you."

Boomer and Dinky had flown in and were listening solemnly to everything Big Mama had to say. They really hoped that Tod would take notice of the wise old owl, for they liked him a lot and didn't want him to get hurt.

"You mean Copper's going to be my enemy?'' said Tod, looking from one to the other of them.

The birds all looked at each other sadly. It seemed there was only one way to make Tod see what danger he could be in if he tried to stay friends with the hound dog.

"Hey, kid,'' said Dinky. "You'd better step over here and take a good look.''

Dinky lead Tod toward the barn door and then, with Boomer's help, he opened it to reveal a wall absolutely covered with animal skins of every description; badgers, rabbits, moles, bears, and . . . foxes!

Tod felt very sick and shook his head, hoping that the terrible sight would disappear. But it didn't.

"Why . . . why that's awful!'' he gasped. "Those poor things!''

Big Mama looked at Boomer and Dinky and nodded for them to close the barn door. She moved quietly over to where Tod was still shaking and put her wing gently around him.

"I'm sorry, Tod, honey. But Copper is going to come back a fully trained hunting dog . . . a real killer.''

"No . . . no . . . not my friend Copper. He won't ever change!'' cried Tod stubbornly.

Big Mama shrugged her shoulders. They had done all they could, now it was up to nature to take its course and only time would tell if Tod was right about his friend. If he wasn't . . .

well, Big Mama didn't like to think about that possibility.

The following months were very lonely ones for Tod. Somehow the fields to run in and the pond to swim in just weren't the same without Copper. Of course, Boomer and Dinky tried to play with him but they didn't enjoy swimming, and rough and tumble was completely out of the question. In fact, if Tod so much as playfully swatted at them they both got very upset and wouldn't come back again for days.

It wasn't long before autumn really took a hold of the countryside, and Tod loved his new found game of chasing the leaves as they dropped from the trees, swirling and dodging in the wind.

One day Tod had been so busy chasing a particularly crafty leaf that he had run straight into the trunk of the tree below, and had raced home to the Widow nursing his aching nose. Another time he had been so busy snuffling around in a lovely soft pile of leaves that he hadn't noticed the new smell that his snout was uncovering, and a furious hedgehog had raced at him, quills bristling; that night the Widow spent quite some time removing the painful needles from Tod's coat.

Soon the trees were completely barren and stood out against the landscape like scarecrows without clothes. Winter was almost with them, and the Widow seemed to spend most of her days chopping and piling up logs for the long winter nights ahead.

Tod would sit and watch her for a while each day, and every time the axe fell, the fox would jump a little bit and make the Widow laugh so much that she had to chase him away before she could continue with her work.

Every morning Tod would look out from the kitchen window at the frost that decorated the buildings and the trees. Little icicles would hang from the window ledges and Tod's first game of the day would be to rush out and break them off, one by one.

He didn't stay out too long now, for the cold wintry winds would drive him in to sit beside the Widow's cozy fire, and the daylight hours were short and precious.

Sometimes Tod would wander over to Slade's property and sniff the empty barrels which still contained the scents of Copper and Chief. He even had a game where he used to pretend that it was a warm summer night and he was going over to collect Copper for some fun and games in the forest while Chief slept on.

Tod would wriggle on his belly through the sparse undergrowth, feeling the ice melting on his coat as he went. Then he would peer over the hill at the two barrels and give one of their secret calls. Slithering down the slope he would run joyfully toward Copper's home and then race around to the front. The game always stopped here because whenever Tod saw the empty barrel and unused blanket he would become so sad that the only thing left to do was go home and try and sleep out the rest of the day.

The first snowfall was fun-filled adventure for Tod. He just couldn't understand what the tiny white pieces were doing, falling from the sky, and spent hours trying to catch one to examine it. But every time he succeeded they would just disappear in his paw and, try though he might, he never found out where they had gone!

But the winter was not so popular with the creatures who didn't have the Widow's cozy house to return to every night.

Poor Squeeks, the caterpillar, dug the deepest hole he possibly could, to try and keep warm, but still his tunnels were covered in frost and he feared every one of his toes would get completely frozen off unless he found somewhere warm soon.

One day Squeeks spotted the lovely glowing light from the Widow's house as she built up the fire to chase away the wintry gloom.

He decided that, somehow, that was the place where *he* was going to spend the winter and started to crawl toward the welcoming light.

His journey had to take him past the Widow's

scarecrow under whose hat Boomer and Dinky were huddling together, hiding from the weather.

"B-r-r-r-r-r-r . . ." shivered Dinky, rubbing his chest furiously. "Jiminies . . . it's sure turned cold!"

It was so cold that the two birds' breath was making a damp fog inside the hat, and they just didn't know what to do to try and stop their beaks from chattering.

"Yeah . . . I'm freezing!" agreed Boomer.

Suddenly, Dinky glanced through one of the holes in the hat and saw something on the ground. He started, completely forgetting how cold he was, and almost knocked poor Boomer off the scarecrow's head.

"Hey!" he cried out, excitedly. "It's that fuzzy worm! Let's get him . . ."

Boomer knew immediately who Dinky meant. He still hadn't forgiven Squeeks for escaping last time and couldn't wait to try and repay him for the indignities he had suffered.

"Charge!!!" cried Dinky, throwing off the hat and taking off at full speed.

But Squeeks had heard the noisy birds in good time and quickly dived into a nearby snowbank in an effort to escape.

Boomer and Dinky threw themselves at the bank, sending great flurries of snow in all directions as their wings dug into the soft white blanket.

Suddenly, Boomer's head appeared from beneath the pile.

"Dinky! Quick! Over here!" he called out, between clenched beak. Boomer then started to heave on something as hard as he could. "I . . . I . . . g-got him!" he spluttered, giving one last final heave.

But it wasn't Squeeks that Boomer pulled triumphantly out from under the snow pile. It was a highly disgusted Dinky, all puffed up and covered with snow!

"Do I look like a worm?" Dinky squawked indignantly. "That's who we're after . . . come on!"

Dinky managed to get himself the right way up and beckoned with his wing for Boomer to follow him.

By this time Squeeks had actually reached the Widow's front door and was attempting to climb up it as fast as all of his legs would carry him.

With a gigantic effort, Squeeks reached the keyhole and threw himself into it, just as his two pursuers had spotted him.

Dinky was the first to reach the door and, holding onto the door with one of his claws, he squinted one eye to peer through the little hole.

"Humph! Will you look at that!"

The sight that met Dinky's eye was one of Squeeks comfortably ensconced on the side of a flowerpot which happened to be near enough to the fire for the little caterpillar to roast all his legs quite thoroughly.

"Why . . . the little creep. Warm and cozy by the fire!"

Squeeks rubbed his several different sets of hands together, and held some of them out again toward the glow from the fire.

Boomer pushed Dinky out of the way, so that he could get a look.

"Let me take a look," he said angrily.

Boomer couldn't believe his eyes. Squeeks had even brought his knitting with him and was by now leaning back and humming quietly to himself.

"H-how do you like that g-guy. As snug as a bug!"

Boomer shivered and looked around at the ice and snow.

"While we're freezing our beaks off!"

Dinky brushed the snow off his wings. It was definitely time they both made tracks for the nice, warm southern place where all sensible birds went for the winter.

"Well . . . yacking and shivering isn't getting us anywhere. Don't worry, Boomer. We'll get that no good worm when we get back," said Dinky, preparing to take flight.

The two birds took one last look at the gloating caterpillar and then they were off, for they had a long journey ahead of them and couldn't afford to wait around any longer.

"So long, Big Mama!" Dinky called out as they flew past Big Mama's tree.

"Yeah . . . we're heading s-south!" Boomer told her, as the owl's face appeared from the hole.

"Goodbye, boys!" Big Mama called out. "See you next spring!"

From the window of the Widow's house, Tod looked out and saw the two birds disappearing. They had told him all about how one day in the winter they would have to leave the valley and fly south until springtime. But he wished they could have stayed to say goodbye to him.

Tod returned to his basket, wondering how much longer the winter could go on. Not long, he hoped, for Big Mama had told him that Copper would be returning in the spring and he couldn't wait to see his friend again.

Far away from the farm, Copper was having a much better time. He was learning so many things and having such a good time that he had almost forgotten poor Tod.

Every morning Slade would wake early and cook himself and the two dogs breakfast on a small stove. Then it was time to annoy old Chief while Slade got things ready for the day's hunting.

At first, the puppy was happy simply to bound along in Slade's footprints, sometimes digging furiously in the snow when a strange new smell caught his attention.

Copper didn't know or care that he was supposed to be working. He loved the snow and even when he fell flat on his face in it and howled loudly as the wet, cold stuff got into his eyes, he soon forgot and went frolicking off again, much to the disgust of old Chief, who often had to go and dig the young rascal out and carry him through the largest and deepest snow drifts in his mouth.

Chief sometimes wondered if Copper was really a hound dog at all, he seemed so uninterested in everything he tried to teach him.

One day Chief found a particularly interesting twig which smelled very strongly of rabbit.

After a good long sniff, Chief left the twig and tried to follow the scent which had been partly obscured by the falling snow.

Copper raced up to the twig and began to sniff too, just like he had seen Chief do many times before. He was just about to gallop off when he suddenly noticed Chief rear up and freeze every muscle.

Chief struck his best hunting pose and growled menacingly.

He had seen a small rabbit busily foraging for food to take home to his family, and the idea of rabbit stew for supper was making his old mouth water good and proper.

Copper followed Chief's gaze and spotted the

rabbit's bobtail dodging about in the snow. Eager to show Chief that he had listened to his teachings, Copper decided that this time he'd show him, and raced off in pursuit of the rabbit.

Chief was just about to spring when Copper raced past and bowled him completely over in the snow. He made such a commotion that the rabbit spotted him immediately and ran off, easily outdistancing the young pup as he gambolled and pushed his way through the snow.

Soon they came to a fallen log and the rabbit hopped over, scampered under the log and was out of sight.

Copper came barreling along and, although he tried very hard indeed, found that he just couldn't stop at the log, and skidded wildly, landing in a heap on a nearby frozen pond.

Chief strolled over and peered at the unfortunate pup, then shook his head in disgust and trotted back to his master, leaving Copper to untangle himself and get back onto the bank as best he could.

Poor Copper tried again and again to imitate Chief's tracking powers, but each time he tried it usually ended in Slade laughing at him till his sides were almost bursting, or getting so cross that he refused to give Copper any supper.

Then, one day, the three of them were out in the forest and Copper just knew that today was going to be it; today was the day when he was going to prove to Slade and old Chief that he was as good a hunting dog as any, even if he died in the process.

Sniffing through the snow enthusiastically, Copper suddenly stopped and rigidly held his hunting pose.

Chief gave him one look and went off in the opposite direction, convinced that it was only another of Copper's silly antics and not to be taken seriously.

Slade was just about to follow in Chief's direction, when Copper suddenly let out an almighty howl as he raced toward a tree.

Amos Slade watched in amazement as a flurry of birds flew out, flushed out by Copper's cries, and in a second had his gun aimed and was bringing them down at a tremendous rate.

When he had bagged as many as possible, Slade raced over to Copper and affectionately rustled his ears this way and that.

"Good boy, Copper. Good dog. I knew you could do it!" praised Slade, as Chief watched from a distance.

From that day on Copper often took the lead when they went out. He became expert at picking up the slightest trail and couldn't wait to be off whenever he saw Slade getting ready for an outing.

Copper never took much notice of the guns or the traps which Slade carried. And even when he helped Slade shoot a bird or an animal, it didn't really upset him. For hunting was in his nature; it gave him such a thrill of excitement when he sniffed out a rabbit warren or a badger's set, that he didn't really notice what happened afterward. Copper was simply growing up into what nature had intended him to be . . . a very good hunting dog and a faithful friend to his master.

At the beginning of the trip old Chief pushed the young pup out of the way whenever there was work to be done, and very often had to go and retrieve him when Copper got stuck in a hollow log or fell down into a deep snow drift. But as time wore on both Chief and Slade realized that Copper was becoming more and more useful, and soon it was Copper who lead the way whenever a new scent or trail appeared.

By the time spring had come around Copper had grown almost as big as Chief, and Slade was as proud as proud could be of his two great hunting dogs. All of them were very sad when eventually it was time to return home, and Copper didn't think once that it would give him his first opportunity in months to see his old friend, Tod.

The coming of springtime at the farm brought grassy fields for Tod to roll in and flowers for him to smell. The Widow had no fears for his safety while Amos Slade was away, and he had become used to roaming free during the day and returning home for his meal and his nice comfortable basket in the evenings.

He had almost become used to being on his own and didn't think about it so much any more, except when he went to swim and could almost hear Copper splashing about beside him like he did when they were young.

One day, Tod was on his way to a nearby meadow when he passed under Big Mama's tree and heard a peculiar kind of brushing noise.

When he looked up he saw a huge pile of old leaves being swept out of her hole. Big Mama was doing her spring cleaning.

Too late, Tod realized that Big Mama hadn't heard him arrive, and with one tremendous final sweep, the whole pile of leaves landed on his head, making him cry out in alarm.

Big Mama flew out of her hole and down to the moving pile of leaves just as Tod poked his head out.

"Well . . . look who's here!" she laughed, brushing the leaves away from the fox. "Oh my goodness! I'm sorry, Tod, honey!"

Tod didn't really mind and was just about to ask if there was anything he could do to help Big Mama, when the sound of wings flapping made them both look up.

It was Boomer and Dinky who had just flown back for the summer.

Big Mama jumped up and down with excite-

ment, and walked over to the fence on which the two birds had landed.

"Hi, Big Mama!" Dinky called out. "We're back! We flew all the way!"

Boomer jumped up and down and nodded in agreement.

"Oh, yes . . . yes . . . we did!" he cried out.

"Welcome home! You know it's been kind of lonesome around here without you boys!" Big Mama said, looking from one to the other of her friends.

"Hi, fellas!"

Tod had walked quietly toward the fence and sat looking up at the three birds.

Boomer pointed toward the fox and frowned.

"Who t-th-that!" he asked in a frightened little voice, for, generally speaking, foxes were not his favorite sort of animal.

Dinky wasn't so worried. He took off and flew around Tod, looking him up and down.

"This can't be that scrawny little thing we found by that fence post, can it?!" Dinky laughed, still circling. "Come on now!"

Boomer rubbed his eyes and breathed a sigh of relief.

"I just don't believe it!" he said in astonishment.

Tod laughed as Dinky circled nearer and nearer; he enjoyed being the center of so much attention.

"It's me alright," he told the two woodpeckers.

"Hey," called out Dinky. "Lookee here . . . . he's got himself a real fancy collar."

Boomer too had taken off and was inspecting his old friend, Tod.

"Yeah . . . and just look at this bushy tail . . . b-b-beautiful!" he cried, lifting Tod's brush in his beak and waving it grandly from side to side.

Big Mama and Dinky giggled helplessly as Boomer suddenly tossed Tod's tail around his neck, for all the world like some big bushy red scarf.

"Aw, cut it out!" cried Tod, trying to release his tail. "You guys are always teasing me!"

Boomer dropped his tail as the sound of the Widow's creaky front door disturbed his antics.

Flying back to the fence to join Dinky and Big Mama, Boomer saw the Widow emerge from her house carrying a very sad looking pot plant that had definitely seen better days.

The Widow put the plant down on the ground. She had decided that the few barren stems that were left on the plant did nothing to adorn her house, and that the best thing was to put the plant outside in the sun and see if it improved.

Suddenly, the well trained eyes of the two birds saw a familiar figure appear over the edge of the pot.

"Look! It's him!" cried Dinky, excitedly. Then he turned to Tod and said, "Look, kid, we'll see you later. Boomer and me's got some unfinished business to take care of."

With that the two birds hastily left the fence and flew off toward the Widow's house and the pot which had been Squeeks the Caterpillar's home for the winter.

"I don't understand," said the Widow sadly. "It was so healthy."

Squeeks had ducked down beneath the soil when he heard her voice. He felt very appre-

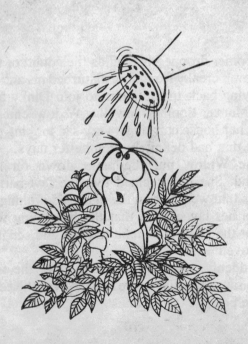

ciative that the Widow had grown such a delicious plant to keep him fed and happy during the winter months, but didn't really think that she would see it that way.

As she turned to go back indoors, Squeeks put out his head and got drowned by a sudden shower of rain.

It was the Widow's watering can as she decided to give the plant one last good soaking before she left.

"There, that ought to perk it up a bit," she said, leaving a very wet caterpillar indeed.

"Ah . . . ah . . . atishoo!" cried Squeeks, who had sneezed so forcefully that he was thrown out of the flowerpot and into the mouth of a nearby drainpipe.

"Where'd he go? Where'd he go?" cried Boomer, as they landed beside the plant.

Dinky looked around and suddenly caught sight of the back end of Squeeks disappearing up the pipe.

"He's going up that drainpipe!" he called out, flying up toward the roof of the house, while Boomer walked over to the bottom of the pipe. "Okay, Boomer. We've got him trapped! Let 'im have it!"

Boomer braced his beak and then started tapping at the metal base of the pipe.

"Rat-a-tat-tat . . . Rat-a-tat-tat . . ." he went.

But Boomer was tapping so hard that the vibrations knocked Dinky completely off his perch at the top end, and just as he was struggling to recover his balance on the roof, Squeeks crawled out of the top of the pipe and along the roof away from his predators.

"Did you get him?" asked Boomer from below.

"NO! Did you?" asked Dinky, rather shaken up from his fall.

"N-no," said Boomer sadly, wondering what had gone wrong up at the top.

Dinky was hopping mad by now and looked this way and that, trying to see the fat little creature.

"Look!" he screeched suddenly, pointing toward some telephone wire.

Squeeks had crawled from the roof onto the telephone wire and was making for the post, meaning to go down it to the ground.

But when he saw Boomer and Dinky flying toward the post to wait for him, he hurriedly turned tail and ducked into the glass insulator, and sat, trembling, wondering what would happen next.

Boomer and Dinky left the post and flew onto the wire which led from the insulator box.

"Ha . . . ha . . . caterpillar under glass . . . ho . . . ho . . . ho," laughed Boomer loudly, thinking that now they really had him trapped.

Poor Squeeks began to tremble even more violently as Boomer prepared his beak to attack the insulator box.

"Rat-a-tat-tat!" he went. "Rat-a-ta . . . ow!!!!"

Suddenly the insulator box shorted out and gave the two birds a rather nasty taste of electricity, singeing their wings and making them leave the telephone wire at double quick speed.

The glass of the insulator box was completely shattered and a rather dazed Squeeks peered out from beneath the remaining shards.

"H-o-l-y s-m-o-k-e!" gasped Boomer, as he reached the safety of the telephone pole. Dinky regarded his friend in horror, for not only were Boomer's feathers a very unattractive shade of black, he was also breathing out smoke, like a burned-out dragon.

Squeeks took the opportunity to climb out of the box and along the wire. He too had got a shot of electricity and appeared to be glowing as he disappeared down onto the roof.

"How'd he do that?" gasped Boomer, still swaying slightly from his shock. "How'd he *do* that!"

But Dinky was gazing far off into the distance where he could see a tiny speck approaching, and he could hear the coughs and splutters of old Slade's truck as it wended its way toward home.

"I ain't got no job. I'm a hunting man and I'd rather have a dog than a dollar, so let's go banjo ringa linga ding . . ."

Amos Slade was singing at the top of his voice as he drove his old truck back toward home. In between verses he glanced back at Chief, who had somehow got relegated to the back of the truck while Copper occupied the prized position of front seat.

"Aw, c'mon, Chief . . . just because you're not sitting up front, that ain't no reason to be a sorehead. Why, if it wasn't for you, old Copper here would never have turned out to be such a good hunting dog."

Chief turned his head away in disgust. Hummph! Good hunting dog indeed! That mongrel was still the no-good whippersnapper he always was, only now he had learned how to get into the master's good books.

Slade leaned back and gave Chief a friendly pat, and Copper tried to reach to lick him. But Chief was having none of it.

"Yessir. Now I've got the best *two* dogs in the whole county. Right, Copper?" Slade removed his beaten-up old hat and placed it at a jaunty angle on Copper's head.

Copper howled with pleasure and nuzzled his master's arm.

"Isn't he something, Chief?" laughed Slade, not noticing that his old dog had placed his

paws over his eyes so he wouldn't have to watch such sycophantic goings-on.

As they neared the farm, word had already reached Tod that Copper and his family were returning, and he was racing up the hill so that he would be able to spot the truck when it appeared on the horizon. He was so excited about seeing Copper again that he could hardly make his legs move fast enough, and his tail stood upright and bushy in greeting.

"Look, Big Mama! Copper's back . . .!" gasped Tod, as the poor old owl tried frantically to keep up with the fox.

Tod and Big Mama settled themselves on a good vantage point and watched as the truck got nearer and nearer the farm, until it eventually came to a rattling standstill outside the door.

Copper leaped from the truck and sat expectantly waiting while Slade lowered himself from the driving seat.

"Boy, has Copper grown big!" exclaimed Tod, his voice full of pride at what a handsome dog Copper had grown into.

But Big Mama was not so proud, or pleased to see Copper.

"Yes, and look at that big pile of skins he helped track down!" Big Mama pointed toward the back of the truck where a grizzly array of all sorts of animal skins were heaped one on top of the other.

"I know, Big Mama," said Tod sadly. "He's a hunting dog now."

"Right! And you're a fox," warned Big Mama, shaking a warning finger at him.

Tod looked pensively down at the scene below and longed to race down and roll in the dust with Copper, just like they used to.

"I've just got to find out if he's still my friend," he said.

Big Mama shrugged. "Well, honey . . . just don't get your hopes too high."

"Look, don't worry . . . I'll be careful. I'll go over tonight when Chief and the Hunter are sound asleep," said Tod, who just couldn't wait for it to get dark now that he had decided what to do.

"Boy! It's great to be back home, isn't it, Chief?" said Copper enthusiastically, rolling deliriously on his back after their evening meal.

"Huh . . . huh," agreed Chief sleepily from the depths of his barrel.

Copper walked over to the front of the barrel and addressed Chief's rear end.

"Aw, c'mon, Chief . . . you aren't still sore, are you!"

Chief turned himself around in his kennel and, head on paws, gazed morosely at Copper, whom he had not yet forgiven for taking his precious place up front in the truck.

"Hey, let's scuffle," said Copper, playfully

swatting one of Chief's ears. "We ain't scuffled in a long time. Come on, Chief, let's have some fun."

Much against his better judgment, Chief found himself beginning to enjoy Copper's puppyish wrestling and even started to join in a little bit.

"Cut it out . . . ah!" Chief laughed, as Copper almost sat on his nose. "Why, you overgrown pup, let go! I say let me go!"

By this time Copper had gone a little bit too far and Chief gave a serious warning growl.

"Okay. Okay." said Copper, slinking sulkily back to his own barrel.

Chief gave his ruffled coat a few soothing licks and tried to regain his dignity.

"You know, that was your trouble on the hunt. There's far too much puppydog still left in you. Smelling and tracking just isn't enough to make a good hunter. You've got to think nasty too!"

Copper breathed a deep sigh. He was just about fed up with Chief treating him like a six-week-old pup, and after all the good tracking he'd done while they were away as well. But he knew better than to try and argue with the older dog, so he simply grunted and settled down to rest, while Chief's head disappeared back into the depths of his barrel.

Later that night, when the moon had risen and the whole valley was bathed in a warm yellow glow, Copper started as he heard some twigs snapping nearby. He lifted his head and his ears tingled expectantly while his nose twitched as a familiar scent wafted toward him on a light breeze.

"Copper . . . pst! Hey, Copper, over here. It's me, Tod."

Cautiously, Tod emerged from behind a bush and stood sheepishly grinning at the now fully awake Copper.

"I thought that was you, Tod. I heard you coming. Boy! You've really grown," said Copper, looking the fox up and down.

"You have too, Copper," said Tod. "I saw you coming back with Chief and the Hunter."

Copper looked slightly uncomfortable. Maybe he didn't like the idea of Tod seeing him return with all the skins.

"It's great to see you, Tod. But you know, you shouldn't be over here. You're . . . you're going to get us both into a lot of trouble."

Tod tried not to notice the rather cold note in Copper's voice, why, he was probably just excited to see him.

"Look, I just wanted to say hello," said Tod. "We're . . . we're still friends. Aren't we?"

Copper looked down toward the ground. He was feeling very awkward, for something had to be said and he didn't really know how to say it without hurting Tod dreadfully.

"Tod, those days are over. I'm a . . . a hunting dog now," said Copper, feeling even worse as Tod looked at him with complete disbelief. "Hey, you'd better get out of here before old Chief wakes up."

"Oh, Chief doesn't worry me," said Tod, trying to act bravely.

"Tod, I'm serious," warned Copper, who had seen the way Chief loved chasing foxes while they were away. "You're fair game as far as he's concerned."

Suddenly, Chief's barrel almost rocked as a tremendous growl emitted from it and Chief's face appeared in the doorway, his teeth bared ferociously.

Tod didn't stop to argue any more and started to run for all his life was worth back toward the Widow's house.

Amos Slade had been woken up by Chief's angry barking and soon appeared in the doorway, gun in hand.

"It's that fox again!" he screeched angrily and, taking aim, began to fire at Tod's retreating brush.

Chief wasted no time in running after Tod, and Copper raced after Chief, not knowing whether he was excited about the prospect of a chase or worried for Tod's safety.

The two dogs were making so much noise that they woke the Widow, and she quickly appeared at her doorway carrying a lantern.

"Oh no, no. They're after Tod!" she cried as the shape of the fox sprang into her view.

"After him, boys, go get him!" the Widow heard Amos Slade call out to his dogs.

Tod threw himself under the fence and over a large log, stumbling as another blast narrowly

89

missed him. He spied some bushes and made for them with Chief close behind. On and on he ran, his sense of direction destroyed by his fear. Around the trees, through a stream, deep, deep into the undergrowth, and still Chief was only a few yards behind him.

A steep hill almost made him give up, but the angry growling from behind forced him to carry on. Soon they came to a railroad and Tod spied a bulky container lying near the tracks. He'd gained a little on Chief and decided that it was worth a try. So he slunk behind the container and waited as Chief ran on, not noticing that the scent had stopped.

Tod breathed deeply. He knew it was only a matter of minutes before Chief turned around and he had to make the most of it.

Before he had expected it a loud sniffing made him turn in alarm.

"Copper! Copper!" The voice of Slade rang out through the night and Copper stared at Tod who cringed back into his once safe corner.

The two animals looked deep into each other's eyes, neither of them knowing what to do, their instincts battling with their memories.

"Copper! Copper!" The Hunter called out again, and the dog turned to see the shape of Slade appearing in the distance. He turned back to the fox.

"Tod . . . I don't want to see you get killed but . . ."

"Track him down, boy!" called out the Hunter.

"Look . . . I'll let you go this one time," whispered Copper. And with that he turned and made off in the opposite direction, letting out a huge howl to draw Slade away from Tod's hiding place.

"Don't lose him!" called out Slade, excitedly running after his dog.

Tod watched them disappear, and slunk out from behind the container. He raced uphill, following the tracks closely, and had just reached the straightaway when a shape leaped down onto the line in front of him. It was Chief, his face a picture of pleasure as he regarded the tired fox.

Tod did an about turn and started back in the direction from which he had come, with Chief snapping at his heels and letting out loud barks and howls.

Amos Slade stopped following Copper and turned toward the noise.

"There they are! Old Chief's got him on the run!" Slade began to run. He was sure that this time he'd be lucky.

Tod had just about reached the top of the hill when his eye was caught by a flash of light in the distance. He kept on running but suddenly realized that the light was an oncoming train and he was on the tracks!

Taking a sideward curve, Tod left the tracks

just before they wound higher with a steep slope on one side and a deep drop on the other.

But Chief was too busy to notice that the fox was no longer on the tracks. In fact, he didn't even notice the oncoming train, or the rumbles and groans that the lines were making beneath his paws.

Amos Slade had noticed though, and stood rooted to the spot as his dog raced toward certain death.

"Jump! Chief, jump!" Slade called out desperately.

Only then did Chief look ahead into the darkness. With a quick glance toward the unclimbable slope on his right, Chief obeyed his master's orders and jumped, closing his eyes as he did so.

Down, down, tumbled the old dog until eventually his body landed with a resounding splash into the shallow river below.

Tod peered down from his hiding place at the top of the hill and watched as Copper and Slade raced toward Chief's still body.

"Chief!" he heard Copper call out, as the young dog sniffed and pawed at the half-submerged head of Chief. But still Chief didn't move.

"Oh no . . . no!" cried Copper and, looking up, let a piteous howl. Suddenly he spied Tod looking down on them and a low growl came from his snarling mouth.

"Tod . . ." Copper called out. "If it's the last thing I do I'll . . . I'll get you for this."

"Tod . . . Tod . . ." This time another, more gentle voice called out of the darkness and Tod glanced behind to see the Widow's waving lantern appearing a little way away.

With one more look down, Tod raced away toward the light and the Widow scooped him up in her arms, just like she used to when he was a cub.

"Oh, Tod! Thank heaven you're safe!" she cried, nuzzling the whimpering fox.

Copper's howling made them both look up, and the Widow clutched Tod even tighter and whispered into his coat, "Something has got to be done."

Chapter 5

With Copper's help, Amos Slade managed to get Chief back to the house. Luckily he had only been knocked unconscious by his fall, and apart from a few very painful bumps and bruises, he was still the same old Chief he used to be.

Copper had been sent outside to sit in his barrel while Slade made Chief a comfortable bed inside the house and heated up some warm soup to make him feel better.

After a little while the door to the house burst open and Slade strode out, clutching his gun.

Copper retreated hastily back into his barrel, not knowing if Slade was aware just how much of what happened had been his fault.

But Amos Slade carried right on walking, toward the lights which burned from the Widow's house.

Boomer and Dinky were sleeping peacefully a few branches above Big Mama's hole, and

Dinky was awakened by the noise of the Hunter's footsteps.

Watching carefully, Dinky decided he'd better do something about this; somehow he knew that Tod was in terrible danger.

"Big Mama! Big Mama!" he cried, flying up and landing in front of her face. "Big Mama, wake up. There's trouble!"

The birds watched as the Hunter stormed up and hammered on the Widow's front door.

Tod had already sensed the danger and had jumped out of his basket and was hiding behind the stove.

"Tod, what is it?" laughed the Widow at the sight of his two big terrified eyes peering out at her.

The hammering continued.

"Widow!" yelled Amos Slade. "You get out here this minute!"

"What on earth . . ." exclaimed the Widow, rushing to the door. She undid the latch and gaped in amazement at the sight of Amos Slade who was almost bursting with anger and brandishing his gun.

"Why . . . Amos . . . Wha——"

"Where is he?" screamed Slade, trying to peer over her shoulder. "I know he's in there."

The Widow had now recovered from her surprise and was beginning to get very irritated by Slade's manner.

"Now just a minute!" she barked back at

him. "You can't come barging onto my property, Amos Slade!"

This time Slade wasn't about to let himself be bullied.

"That fox of yours almost killed Chief!" he screamed, his nose about an inch away from the Widow's face. "And I'm going to get him!"

The Widow had had quite enough of this treatment and shoving the Hunter backward, she slammed the door in his face and bolted the latch.

"You can't keep him locked up forever!" called out Slade from the other side of the door. But for the moment at least, Tod was safe.

Boomer, Dinky and Big Mama had watched

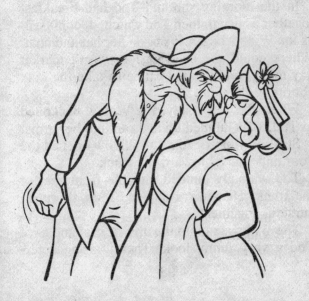

all this going on and silently cheered at the Widow's actions. But Slade was right, she couldn't keep a fox locked up in a house forever; not only would that be cruel but, knowing Tod, it would also be impossible.

Slade paced up and down the Widow's front garden for about half an hour then, muttering, turned and headed for home, vowing that "that fox's" days were numbered.

The rest of the night the Widow rocked quietly in her chair, while Tod slept uneasily in his basket. She seemed to be in deep thought and, now and then, would look toward the little photograph of Tod as a cub which was hanging on the wall, and wipe away a tear.

In the morning she and Tod had breakfast together as usual, then Tod watched, confused, as the Widow began to put on her hat and coat. Where could she be going? It wasn't market day today, and it wasn't time to take the milk churns to the dairy.

When she was ready, the Widow beckoned to Tod, who jumped up and ran into her arms.

Still carrying the fox, the Widow opened the door and started toward the truck.

Tod willingly jumped into the front seat of the truck. He always enjoyed their short excursions together.

The Widow got into the driving seat and gave Tod a very funny look. Then, staring determinedly ahead at the road, she began to drive much faster than usual toward wherever they were going.

As they passed the Hunter's house, Amos Slade was walking toward his door carrying a load of wood. Hearing the Widow's engine, Amos stopped and peered curiously at the fox staring out from the side window. Now, he wondered, where could the Widow woman be off to with that murdering creature?

Above the truck two woodpeckers circled and dipped as though following the vehicle.

It was Boomer and Dinky who had strict instructions to report Tod's whereabouts at all times to Big Mama, who was very worried since the happenings of the night before.

Inside the cab, the Widow was looking lovingly at Tod and talking quietly to herself. From the snatches he could hear, Tod thought she seemed to be remembering their very first meeting and how she had fed him milk from a make-do bottle.

Occasionally the Widow would laugh when she recalled the games they used to play and the mischief Tod would get into almost every day. But then her voice changed and she began to look so sad that Tod wished he could cheer her up, and he put a paw tenderly upon her arm.

"Goodbye may seem forever, Tod. But always remember, you'll always be with me, in my heart and my memories."

Tod gazed up at the Widow mournfully; he didn't understand what was happening at all. Where could they be going to, so far away from home? And why were the Widow's eyes leaking all the time?

He looked out at the surrounding countryside. It certainly was beautiful here, specially down the tiny little lane into which the Widow had only just turned. Deeper and deeper into the forest they drove, until finally the Widow pulled off the road slightly and stopped the truck.

She turned off the engine and clambered down from her seat. Coming around to Tod's side of the truck, she opened the door and gathered him in her arms. Tod would have preferred to walk, there was such beautiful springy moss on the ground and such wonderful new smells everywhere. But he didn't want to upset the Widow any more so he lay quietly in her arms as she walked further and further into the depths of the forest.

At last she stopped walking and looked around her as though inspecting the area. Tod gave her a great enormous lick down one side of her face and the huge hug which the Widow gave him nearly took his breath away. When the hugging was over she leaned down and set him on the ground.

Without a word, she turned and began to walk back in the direction of the truck, so Tod decided he'd better follow her.

The Widow turned and shook her head, her eyes leaking really badly again. "No, Tod. Not this time."

Tod sat down again. Surely she couldn't actually mean to leave him here? Exciting though this new place was, he didn't want to be left here all alone.

But the Widow walked on and not once did she turn around to call him.

Tod watched as the tiny figure of the Widow finally reached the truck. She got in very slowly and peered out through the window at the still figure of the animal she loved so much. But she knew that Tod's very life would be in danger if she gave in and took him home. So she resolutely started up the truck and drove off as fast as she could without a second look around.

Tod shivered as a sharp wind suddenly blew up, rustling the trees of the forest and making an eerie whistling sound above his head. A storm was beginning to brew and Tod jumped nervously as lightning streaked across the sky. Another flash and Tod was running toward the cover of some leafy bushes from which he peered out as the other animals of the forest began to run for cover too.

A brown squirrel ran toward the tree under which Tod was sheltering and, scampering up

the trunk, ran along a low hanging branch and sprang across to his nest, sending a shower of raindrops pouring down onto Tod's head.

The fox shook himself crossly and decided to try and find a drier place to stay. Soon he found quite a large hole about two feet from the ground in an old gnarled oak tree.

Tod climbed up and gingerly stuck his nose into the hole. But a warm dry smell of fur and food warned him that the hole was occupied, even before he saw the family of racoons staring up at him from their snug little home.

Unknown to Tod, a friendly pair of eyes had

been watching him as he looked for a place of refuge from the rain.

"Oh, what a shame. I bet he's a stranger and got no place to stay," said Mr. Porcupine to himself as Tod turned sadly away from the hole.

More lightning zipped through the forest and Tod started to run in blind fear. He *had* to find somewhere out of this storm.

At the foot of a tree a large gaping hole seemed to beckon to him as he ran, but as soon as Tod's head was inside the hole he found himself nose to nose with a *very* unfriendly badger.

"Hold it sonny! Back off! Where in tarnation do you think you're going to?"

The badger shoved Tod rudely toward the outside of his set.

"Oh . . . oh . . . excuse me. I . . . I . . . I . . . I was, I was just trying to . . ."

"You barge in on somebody's house like you own it," shouted the badger, shoving Tod some more. "Tarryhooting around them woods, waking up folks in the middle of the night."

Tod blinked. He was sure it was still daytime. He didn't know that, to a badger, who sleeps all day and hunts all night, daytime was nighttime.

"I honestly didn't know anybody lived here, and I . . ." Tod tried to explain again.

But the badger was having none of it. "Well, you know now! So get off my property. Go on

. . . beat it!'' snarled the badger, moving in for another shove.

Tod continued to apologize as he backed out of the hole. Suddenly he found his rear end stinging rather painfully.

The Porcupine had followed Tod and had been listening to the argument outside the badger's hole.

Tod moved sideways and rubbed the spot where the quills had pricked him, while Mr. Porcupine giggled guiltily.

"I have been watching you, sir," said the Porcupine, recovering from his fit of giggles. "You can stay with me if you want."

Tod looked over the prickly little animal and thought better of the idea.

"Oh, well . . . look, that's very nice of you, but . . . ah . . . Oh I think I've just seen a place . . . right over there. Thanks just the same." And with that, Tod moved away toward a nearby cave he had just spotted.

The Porcupine frowned beneath his quills. That silly fox was going to get himself into even more trouble, he just knew it.

And the Porcupine was right. For just as Tod flopped down beside what he thought was a very convenient rock, the rock opened its eye and suddenly turned into a huge bear who was not exactly over pleased at the arrival of this uninvited visitor.

The bear let out an enormous roar of anger

and Tod was off like a shot. He didn't need to be told twice!

Outside the cave the Porcupine was still waiting to see what would happen, and a very embarrassed Tod decided to ask if his offer was still open.

"Oh yes, you're more than welcome," said the Porcupine, who was very lonely and hadn't got many friends. "Come with me."

Tod followed the Porcupine through the forest, keeping well back from the dangerous quills. By now it was beginning to get dark and Tod was feeling very tired.

"Here, you can sleep in my bed. It's nice and warm," said the Porcupine kindly when they reached his house.

Tod flopped down onto the bed and fell asleep almost immediately.

"After a good night's sleep things will look much better in the morning," said the Porcupine, settling down himself into a large, comfy chair.

But after an hour or so Tod woke up. He was missing his old basket and the warm smell of cooking which always seemed to hang around the Widow's kitchen. He didn't like this strange forest and he liked the animals in it even less. If only his friends Dinky and Boomer and Big Mama were here, they would know what to do, thought Tod, who spent the rest of the night tossing and turning in an uneasy dreamfilled sleep in which he dreamed Copper was his friend again and the two of them were swimming and playing in the pond, just like they used to.

"Tod! Tod!" A worried call echoed through the early morning forest as Big Mama looked this way and that trying to find the missing fox.

The old owl landed in a rather ungainly way on a branch and puffed noisily.

"Oh boy! These old wings aren't what they used to be. Big Mama, you'd better lose a few pounds in weight before you try this kind of flying again." Suddenly the owl spotted the glint of a red-brown coat through the trees. "Oh . . . oh . . . oh . . . there he is . . . there he is. Tod! Tod!"

Big Mama took off again and flew down between the trees to land on a branch near the fox.

"Oh, hello, Big Mama." Two big brown eyes peered up at the old owl as the little lady fox looked up to see her visitor.

"Oh, it's you, Vixey!" said Big Mama sadly.

"What brings you all this way from home?" asked the little fox curiously, for Big Mama was a very infrequent visitor to the forest.

"I'm looking for a fox named Tod. He's new here in the forest."

Vixey turned around and looked up, interested.

"New? Hmmm . . . well, what does he look like?"

"Oh, he's young and about your age. Very handsome," said Big Mama, who couldn't help noticing that the young vixen was getting more and more excited with her every word.

"Handsome? Oh, well . . . er . . . I'm not doing anything. I'll help you find him," said

Vixey, circling Big Mama's tree, as though she couldn't wait to get going.

Big Mama laughed and took off again. "Come along then, honey. He's got to be around here somewhere."

Inside his home, the Porcupine was beginning to stir at the call of the brand new day. He'd completely forgotten that he had a visitor and began his usual enormous stretch which spanned from one side of his hole to the other. The trouble was, this time Tod was in the way.

"Ow!" cried Tod, as a number of the quills began to stab him painfully in the head.

In his terror Tod panicked and fell out of bed, hitting his head and landing on yet more Porcupine quills. The two of them began to do a silly kind of dance as they tried to avoid each other in the confined space, until eventually Tod fell backward out of the hole and landed, although he didn't know it, at the other entrance to the badger's set.

"Wha-What happened? Where am I?" Tod cried out.

He was quickly about to find out.

"So!" screamed the angry badger, who had just returned from his night out and wanted very badly to go to sleep. "It's you again, eh! You barged in on me last night and now you . . ."

Tod had jumped quickly out of the hole and

was trying hard not to tremble so much. "I . . . I didn't mean to," he stuttered.

Suddenly the badger's home turned into a pile of earth and rocks as the ceiling and sides caved in where Tod had fallen.

"Just look at this mess you've made!" cried the badger, beside himself with frustration. "Dadratit you clumsy bonehead!"

"I'm sorry. It was an accident," Tod cried.

"Bah! Excuses . . . excuses!" yelled the badger.

"Mr. Digger, sir . . . it really was an accident," said the Porcupine who was coming down the tree to Tod's defense.

"You keep out of this . . . you walking pincushion!" said the badger, striding threateningly over to this new intruder.

The Porcupine began to climb up the tree again, thinking that it would be just a little bit foolish to stay on the ground when the badger was in such a dreadful mood.

"Ah . . . you . . . you shouldn't be so grumpy to someone who's new in the neighborhood," called out the Porcupine as a parting shot.

The badger turned back to deal with Tod again.

"A stranger, eh? Well, why don't you go back where you came from? Well, go on . . . get going . . . git, I say!" And with that the badger raised a very dangerous looking paw and Tod decided he'd better "git' as quickly as he could, and ran away without even having time to say "thank you' to the Porcupine for his night's rest.

Finally, Tod stopped running and slowed to a very dejected walk. He was hungry and thirsty and lonely. Oh, why had the Widow done this to him?

A little way away, Big Mama and Vixey had spotted their prey.

"Oh gosh . . . he seems so . . . I don't know . . . so downhearted, Big Mama," said Vixey at the sight of Tod.

"Well, you can't blame him, honey. You see, he was just dropped here and left all alone without a friend in the world," said Big Mama, parting the bushes with her wing and peering through at the sad figure before her.

Vixey stopped staring at the other fox and turned to Big Mama.

"Maybe there's something I can do . . . you know . . . cheer him up," she said.

Suddenly Big Mama seemed to perk up. She shook her wings and blinked her eyes wisely. It might just work . . .

"Honey, you just said the magic words!" Big Mama exclaimed.

The big owl ushered Vixey to a clearing in the forest and whispered something into her ear.

"Oh, big Mama, I don't know . . . I . . ."

"Darling, don't move an inch," ordered Big Mama. "You look beautiful!"

The little fox preened herself at this; she always made a point of keeping her coat clean and her tail neatly brushed.

"Thank you."

Then Big Mama flew off toward where Tod was sitting dejectedly pawing a clump of daisies.

"Morning, Tod," she cried out as she reached him.

"Oh hello, Big Mama," said Tod, relieved to see somebody he knew.

"Last night was pretty miserable for you wasn't it, honey?" asked the owl.

"Just terrible," agreed Tod.

Big Mama wrapped a consoling wing around the fox. "Well, cheer up and look around. The forest is beautiful this morning."

At first Tod wasn't a tiny bit interested in the wretched forest. But after more encouragement from Big Mama, he took a deep breath and looked around him.

Big Mama waited expectantly and then suddenly noticed Tod's mouth drop wide open in astonishment.

"Wow!" Tod breathed after nearly a minute of silence.

"Who . . . who is *that?*"

Big Mama brushed a piece of twig from one of her wings and shrugged non-committedly.

"Oh, just another fox . . . a *lady* fox!" she added, watching Tod's face with pleasure.

"Golly . . . is she beautiful. I wonder what her name is."

At that moment Vixey turned around and gave him one of her prettiest smiles so that Tod blushed the deepest shade of red underneath his thick coat.

"Well, why don't you go and ask her?" prompted Big Mama, giving Tod a gentle prod.

"Yeah . . . yeah . . . I guess I will," said Tod, walking hesitantly off in Vixey's direction. "Ah . . . I'll just go up to her and I'll say . . . 'You're the most gor——' No . . . no . . . that's not right. Er . . . 'I've never seen anybody quite as won——' "

By this time Tod had almost reached Vixey's side and his heart was thumping so much that he wasn't really sure he would be able to say anything at all.

Vixey sat up and waited patiently as her admirer approached.

"H . . . hi!" gasped Tod.

"Hello," said Vixey in a friendly sort of voice. That did it—suddenly they both started talking ten to the dozen and both ended up in fits of giggles, after which Vixey managed to splutter that Big Mama had told her all about Tod.

"May I call you by your first name?" asked

113

Tod politely, as he stared very impolitely into the most beautiful brown eyes he had ever seen.

"Oh . . . oh . . . sure, why not?" said Vixey, but she forgot to tell him what it was.

Tod smiled at her forgetfulness. "Uh . . . thanks. But what is your first name?"

Big Mama watched, a delighted look on her face as the two young foxes exchanged names. They seemed to be getting on really well, just as she had hoped. Maybe now Tod wouldn't feel so alone and lost in the big forest.

"It looks like that farm boy is making a hit with her," laughed Boomer who had just flown in to watch the scene.

Big Mama grabbed his beak between her

claws and clamped it tight shut. She didn't want anything to go wrong with her little piece of matchmaking.

"Now just keep it down," she warned him, as Dinky made sure his beak was well out of reach.

"Uh . . . Tod . . . you know something?" said Vixey, moving slowly toward a nearby

stream. "This stream is just full of trout. Do you think you could catch one?"

"One what?" said Tod, who was still much too busy admiring Vixey to notice anything about his surroundings.

"Fish. Silly!" cried Vixey, giggling.

Tod looked from her to the stream and finally got the message.

"Oh . . . yeah, of course. A fish .. why, my dear young lady, you happen to be looking at an expert *fisher* fox," boasted Tod, confidently jumping onto a nearby floating log. He just about managed to keep his balance as he gingerly stepped along the log to the end.

Oh, Tod, thought Big Mama, you really must stop showing off, it'll only end up in more trouble.

But Tod was enjoying himself now and was out to impress this beautiful female at any cost.

"Oh yes, I know all the tricks . . . in fact, I never miss," said Tod, still swaying precariously on the end of the log.

"Please let him catch a fish," prayed Big Mama, her wings clasped together and her eyes heavenward.

"Oh . . . oh . . . here comes a whopper!" called out Tod. "Now, watch closely."

Tod raised an arm while still balancing on the log with his other paws. Then, quick as a flash, he'd scooped up the fish and thrown it toward the shore. Straight into Vixey's face!

She would have been very cross indeed as the fish had made her soaking wet, but a second later she watched as Tod completely lost his balance and went plunging into the bubbling water, closely following the fish who had bounced straight back.

"Tod . . . do you need help?" Vixey called out, as Tod, still determined to catch the wretched fish, pawed madly at the water around him and tried to keep his head above water.

"No . . . no . . . I . . . I always fish this way . . . Ah!"

Tod failed to catch the fish for the fourth time and then suddenly realized that he had something firmly clenched between his teeth. Thinking it must be the trout, he emerged dripping from the water, ready to present his trophy to Vixey.

"I've got him! he cried and Vixey broke into a huge belly laugh which made Tod drop the stick and suddenly notice that Vixey wasn't the only one amused by his antics. For there were Boomer and Dinky, Big Mama, and Porcupine, and lots of other forest animals, all grinning away at his misfortune. He felt very cross and highly embarrassed and Vixey didn't seem to care one jot.

"Oh . . . oh, Tod. You're the funniest thing I ever saw!" she gasped, holding her sides.

"Go ahead . . . go ahead and laugh, you're

117

just like everyone else around here," snapped Tod, shaking the water from his soggy coat.

"I'm sorry, I can't help it. You were so funny," said Vixey, trying not to laugh any more, and not succeeding very well.

"So . . . I can't fish . . . why, you're a silly, empty-headed female," Tod retorted, his feelings really hurt.

"Now just a minute . . ." said Vixey, beginning to get angry with him. "I mean, you've got nerve. Why don't you just grow up?!"

Big Mama decided that the time had come to intervene. Unless she did so, and quickly, she could see the beginning of the end of a beautiful friendship.

"Tod!" she called out sharply. "That's no way to talk to Vixey."

Tod looked up at the owl through his soaking fur and growled slightly. "Raspberries! I've had it!"

"Honey, don't stay mad," soothed Big Mama, stroking Tod's back. "You've got to be natural, that's the trick."

Tod looked over his shoulder to where Vixey was sitting, stubbornly refusing to look in his direction.

Big Mama looked from one to the other in absolute distraction. It seemed like all her plans were being laid to waste because of one silly little incident.

"Tod . . ." she tried again. "You can't really blame Vixey for laughing, you know. After all, you had claimed to be an expert fisher fox and look what happened! Everyone at some time or another wants to impress somebody else, but believe me, Tod, you'd impress Vixey a

whole lot more if you just acted like your nor-
mal, lovable self.''

Tod was beginning to look very sad and feel
very foolish about his empty boasting. He
hadn't actually meant to lie about his fishing
abilities. But somehow it had just slipped out
and now the beautiful lady fox would probably
not want anything more to do with him. Tod
raised his head and found himself staring into
Vixey's liquid brown eyes. Maybe all was not
lost after all.

Tod tried a smile, but immediately Vixey
turned her head sharply away and began to
study the leaves above her head intently.

Big Mama nodded encouragingly at Tod, as
though she really thought that, despite all he
had done, Vixey might be won over again. But
Tod knew better and, head down, started to
leave the little clearing. Just as he got to the
edge of the trees, he spotted a patch of sweet
smelling blue flowers. Suddenly an idea hit him
and with a quick glance backward to make sure
Vixey wasn't looking, he bent down and picked
one of the flowers between his teeth.

Hesitantly, he turned and made his way back
to where the other fox was cleaning one of her
paws. Several times he felt like running away,
but Big Mama kept nodding and smiling at him,
so he decided to give it one last try.

Actually, Vixey had already seen Tod coming toward her, flower in mouth. But she

wanted to let him suffer just a little bit longer for his stupidity, so she pretended not to notice him until he was standing directly in front of her.

Tod held out his flower for Vixey's inspection and, smiling slightly, Vixey leaned forward to smell it. But the lovely flower was completely full of pollen, and as soon as Vixey got near it she felt a sneeze thundering its way toward her nose.

"Ah . . . . ah . . . . atishoo!" she cried, blowing the pollen all over Tod, which in turn produced the most enormous sneeze from him too.

They smiled at each other coyly and Vixey licked some of the pollen from Tod's cheek. The fish, the argument and Big Mama forgotten, the two animals nuzzled and licked each other affectionately. A small chuckle came from the branch overhead as Boomer and Dinky watched the two lovers. Big Mama quickly flew up and boffed Boomer on the beak, she wasn't having anything else disturb her protégés. Then she left the branch and summoned the two birds to come away with her.

"But, Big Mama," protested Boomer. "It's just getting interesting!"

"Shhhh!" cried Big Mama, chasing them both away, together with the Porcupine and the disgusted badger, who had also been observers to the recent happenings.

"Tod, I just know you're going to love the forest. Listen, why don't I show you around," whispered Vixey, completely oblivious to anything except her newfound friend.

"Sure," replied Tod, who could think of no better way to spend an afternoon.

Vixey showed Tod all the very best spots of the forest. The many little streams and sparkling fresh water to drink, the clearings where the sun played peep-bo with the trees and where the moss and lichen made the most comfortable places to rest, and every now and again she would stop and show him where one of her friends or acquaintances lived, in a tree or down a hole.

Suddenly a family of quail crossed the path in front of them and Vixey smiled as she counted all the baby quail trailing behind their mother.

"One, two, three, four, five, six, seven . . . oh . . . look!"

The last little bird was the comedian of the family and almost fell over as he pecked and chirped at his surroundings.

"Oh, I think six would be just right," breathed Vixey dreamily, thinking aloud.

"Six?" queried Tod, not knowing what she was talking about.

Vixey turned and gave him a kind of secret look.

"Six what?" asked Tod, tailing after her.

Vixey giggled frustratingly. He'd find out soon enough. She was sure that Tod would make a very good father indeed.

Chapter 6

All the way back home the Widow couldn't stop herself crying at the thought of poor Tod left all alone in the forest.

Several times she stopped the truck and contemplated going back to fetch him. But then she thought of Amos Slade's dangerous threats and knew that she must not put Tod's life in danger by keeping him. He was still a wild animal, even though he had been reared in captivity, and she was sure that, after a little while, he would learn to survive in the safety of the game reserve.

As her truck neared home two pairs of eyes anxiously watched to see if Tod was still with her.

Amos Slade and Copper had been waiting a long time for her return and when they spotted the truck they sneaked over toward the Widow's house and watched as she alone got down from the truck's cabin.

"Well, I reckon she dropped that fox off in the game reserve," whispered Slade to Copper. "We'll get him now, that's for sure."

Copper looked up at his master as a huge streak of lightning lit up his face and its evil grin.

Copper still hadn't forgotten or forgiven Tod for what had happened to Chief, but he didn't like the look of Amos Slade's face at all, and shivered, hoping he'd soon be allowed back to the safety of his nice warm barrel.

Back inside the Hunter's house old Chief was having himself an absolute whale of a time.

His fall had resulted in one broken leg and one very shocked and winded dog for about half an hour. Once his leg had been fixed and bandaged up, old Chief felt just dandy. But he wasn't letting on to Slade or Copper that he felt fine. No, sirree! By letting them think he was still a poorly invalid, he was given all the best food and allowed to sleep on a nice soft cushion indoors instead of outside with Copper. Yes, Chief was definitely getting a taste of being "ill" and meant to continue for as long as possible.

Chief had watched as Copper and Slade went over to see the Widow's return. He was certainly glad that *he* didn't have to go traipsing around in that storm. Brrr! It was enough to make your tail drop off.

Through the window, Chief saw that the pair

were returning to the house. Quickly he left his vantage point and returned to his nice rug and cushion by the fire, pretending that he'd never moved an inch.

"Well, now, if you're going to have a busted leg this is the way to do it," he chuckled, circling once then settling down. "Good food, soft pillow, warm stove . . . sure beats sleeping in that barrel."

Footsteps approached the door and Chief put on his most pained expression.

"Well, now, here come visitors to see the invalid," he thought to himself, and started to give low moanings and groanings to make sure that anyone within earshot would be in no doubt as to how much he was suffering.

Chief noticed Slade and Copper walk right past the door to his room without even so much as a passing glance. This was no way to treat an invalid.

"How do you like that?" he grunted. "They didn't even ask how I'm feeling . . . huh!"

Chief lumbered to his feet and wandered across to the room where Slade was hanging his coat behind the door. Pushing through into the room Chief let out an earsplitting howl, followed by a very authentic low moan, just to keep them on their feet.

"Chief, get back in there before I break your other leg!"

The old dog turned, satisfied that at last he'd received some attention, however grudging.

Amos Slade began to poke around in the depths of an old cupboard. Now that he knew where that dratted fox was hiding out, he didn't intend to waste any time in getting him good and proper.

Finally he withdrew something from the cupboard and stared at it, a huge grin spreading from ear to ear.

"Copper!" he called out. "Copper, look here."

Copper bounded into the room and sniffed around Slade's trousers.

Slade bent down and showed the heavy iron object to Copper, who didn't like the smell of this thing one little bit.

"Now . . ." said Slade, forcing open two gigantic metal bars covered with evil-looking teeth. "When that fox comes traipsing along, suspecting nothing . . ."

And, winking an eye at the apprehensive Copper, Slade pushed the end of a stick in between the metal jaws which suddenly clamped shut, so hard that they completely shattered the stick.

Copper leaped back in terror, and tried not to think about what would happen to a living paw or leg trapped tight within those bars.

Slade spent the rest of the night polishing and oiling the trap so that it would work smoothly and without a hitch. He told Copper that to-morrow was the big day, the last day for Tod, and that they would both be able to be in on the kill.

NO HUNTING said a big white sign at the entrance to the forest game reserve.

Amos Slade chuckled as he read those words.

"No hunting! Well . . . now . . . we ain't going to do none of that," he said. "Are we, Copper?"

Copper looked up at the iron trap which Slade carried in his arms and waited for an explanation.

"Nope! We're just going to get us a no-good fox."

Slade pulled his pair of wire cutters from his pocket and snipped easily through the fence which surrounded the game reserve. He made a hole just large enough for himself and Copper to squeeze through.

"Alright, boy, get tracking!" he ordered, once they were both in, and Copper's nose started twitching immediately as he sniffed here and there among the undergrowth.

"Smell it out," encouraged Slade, and was rewarded by the suddenly wagging tail of Copper as he started off on a very hopeful scent through the forest.

For some way, Slade followed on Copper's heels; he hoped the young dog wasn't leading

him astray again as he had done that time near the railway tracks.

But Copper seemed very sure of himself this time, and stopped only once to rest his front paws on top of a rock and sniff the air, before heading on further and further into the forest.

The trail lead him right up to the Porcupine's home where Tod had spent his first night, and Copper stopped to investigate the now quite old scent. The Porcupine stuck his head out of the hole, about to welcome a new arrival, but as soon as he saw Copper he shrank back into the safety of his home. He'd heard some terrible stories about hunting dogs and didn't want to get involved with one at all.

Copper found the trail that led away from the Porcupine's hole and started following it eagerly toward the nearby stream where Tod had performed his amazing fishing trick.

Sniffing around the rocks, Copper began to get rather worried that maybe he had lost the trail, or that the stream had washed away the scent.

Up and down he went, nose furiously poking here and there, looking for some clue as to where the fox had gone next. But all sorts of other confusing smells kept getting in his way.

Suddenly his whole body went rigid, and having one last humdinger of a sniff, Copper let out a bloodcurdling howl.

"What have you got there, boy?" cried

Slade, rushing over to view the ground where Copper stood.

Very quickly he spotted the tracks of the fox, and Copper continued to growl.

"Good work!" praised Slade. "He'll be coming right through here heading for water. But he *won't* be drinking any!"

Far away in the forest Tod and Vixey emerged from their new burrow in which they had set up home together. Tod felt that he'd never been so happy in the whole of his life.

"What a great day to be alive, Vixey!" he cried, looking around at the sun dappled forest.

Vixey nuzzled him gently. She was very happy too, never had she dreamed that she would find such a handsome mate.

"Oh, Tod. Me too!" she breathed.

Scampering and rolling together as they went, Tod and Vixey left the burrow to go to the stream for water, giggling all the way.

"That does it!' cried Amos Slade, regarding his handiwork of hiding the trap, which had taken quite some time. "Amos, you crafty old coot. The Devil himself couldn't have done better."

He rufled Copper's ears and looked around him. Now all they had to do was wait.

"Tod . . ." said Vixey slowly as they neared the part of the forest to which they were heading. "Tod, wait a minute."

Vixey was looking around her as though spooked. But Tod had seen or heard nothing.

"What is it, Vixey?" he asked, concerned.

"I don't want to go in there . . . it's too quiet," said Vixey in a frightened, small voice. She moved up closer to Tod and whimpered slightly, glancing all the time this way and that.

"Ah . . . Vixey," said Tod, who put it all down to the inventive imagination which he knew Vixey possessed.

Tod tried to urge her into the forest, but she trembled as though she could almost hear the cruel words of Amos Slade as he sprinkled the final few concealing leaves over the waiting trap.

"There, we'll come back in the morning and find us a trapped fox," he laughed to Copper.

But Copper wasn't listening. His ears were cocked and his nose twitching slightly as he peered into the distance. He wasn't sure . . . but possibly . . . yes . . . yes . . . it definitely was.

Copper gave a low, long growl and Slade raised his hand to shield his eyes as he looked toward where Copper was staring.

Now even he could see the figures of the two foxes, and the Hunter gave a little jump of pleasure that his prey should be arriving so soon.

"He's heading this way," he whispered excitedly to Copper.

"Tod . . . be careful . . ." warned Vixey, as Tod insisted on going on down the path.

Against all her instincts Vixey decided to follow him, jumping at every loose twig and every footfall on the ground.

Suddenly Tod too heard a noise and leaped at least three feet sideways as a leaf floated innocently down onto the ground. Phew! He breathed again, and proceeded cautiously toward the stream, not seeing Amos Slade and Copper concealed behind some bushes.

Slade watched as the fox walked obligingly

toward his trap, and could hardly contain himself as Tod's leg hovered dangerously over the very spot where the wicked iron jaws waited beneath the leaves to snap and tear into his leg.

But Tod had sensed danger at last and stood, one paw held in the air, directly above the trap.

Slade could stand it no longer. He decided to take a shot and give up on the idea of the trap. Slowly and carefully he cocked his gun.

"Click!" went the mechanism, and Tod froze, every sense screaming at him to get out of that place.

Nervously, he began to back up. But as he moved he disturbed the undergrowth surrounding the trap and "CRASH!" the jaws sprang together, catching nothing but air.

Tod sprang as high as he could and then, as soon as his feet touched down, began to run and run, blindly, panic-stricken, away from the dreadful place.

It took Slade a second to realize that his prey was getting away. Then, realizing there was no need for silence any more, he too leaped up from his hideaway and began firing wildly at the retreating fox.

Vixey, who had been waiting for Tod at the entrance to the forest, was trembling uncontrollably by now. She wanted to run too, but she refused to leave without Tod and so forced herself to stay put. "Bang . . . bang . . . bang!"

went Slade's gun, and with every bullet Vixey became more and more terrified.

Tod was coming toward her at breakneck speed, with Copper hot on his heels.

Seeing a hollow log, Tod ran through it hoping to shake Copper off the scent. But Copper was game for anything now, and followed Tod into the log, bullets smashing and crashing around them.

"Dad blast it! He's getting away!" screamed Amos Slade in fury.

"Quick! Vixey!" called out Tod as he reached his mate, and together they raced away, desperately trying to escape the pursuing dog.

As they came over a hill, Tod realized that they had been able to gain a little on Copper and decided it was time to split up.

"Go on," he urged an unwilling Vixey. "Head for the burrow."

With one last look at Tod, Vixey ran off, leaving Tod to face the enraged Copper.

The fox climbed up onto a rock and crouched, waiting for the dog to appear.

After a couple of seconds Copper appeared, barking, over the brow of the hill. He stopped, seeming to sense that it was no longer necessary to keep running. A low growl came from deep inside his throat as he realized that his enemy was right there, behind him, ready to fight.

Tod threw himself down from the rock and lunged at Copper; taking a savage bite at his neck he jumped clear again, knowing that to stay would mean certain death.

Running hard toward his burrow, Tod could almost feel Copper's breath on his heels. It was uphill all the way and Tod was not at all sure that he was going to make it.

But then he saw the welcoming hole and dived in, much to Copper's frustration.

The poor dog began digging madly with his paws. He was much too large to follow Tod, so the only other alternative was to dig him out. Stones and soil were going everywhere, and it was difficult to make out Copper's front paws, they were going so fast.

Inside the burrow Tod panted his way toward a waiting Vixey.

She was so relieved to see him and had just started to nuzzle him welcomingly, when Copper's muzzle appeared at the entrance to the burrow. A horrible growl echoed down through the earth and Tod and Vixey realized that Copper was making the hole bigger by the second.

They stared at each other in sheer panic. Then, with one accord they both turned to make for the rear exit, which they had built for emergencies.

Cautiously Tod stuck his head through the hole, and Vixey squeezed hers up beside him.

"Tod!" she cried.

Tod turned toward the horizon and his stomach turned as he saw the Hunter appear over the brow of the hill, his rifle aimed directly at the burrow.

The two foxes dived back into the burrow, narrowly missing the gun shot that screeched past the hole.

Slade had seen them too and as soon as he reached the burrow he poked his rifle as far into the hole as possible and begun firing as fast as he could.

Tod and Vixey dodged from one side of the tunnel to the other as bullets followed them along. Without thinking, they were racing back to the other entrance, but as soon as it came into sight both of them skidded to a halt in shock. For Copper had very nearly succeeded in making the hole big enough to squeeze through, and his massive paws were still scrabbling away, sending showers of earth all around in his excitement.

Bravely, Tod waited for the right moment then leaped in and bit Copper's paw soundly.

The paw disappeared very quickly and Copper howled in pain as he nursed his wound. But soon the howling stopped and the hound dog was even more furious than before and started to dig again, this time harder and faster than ever.

The two foxes retreated to the middle of their

tunnel and leaned against each other for support. It looked like they were trapped and the chances of getting out of there alive were very slim indeed.

At the other end of the tunnel, Amos Slade was busily making a small bonfire of grass and weeds. When he had a nice big pile, he took out some matches from his pocket and struck one, shielding it from the slight breeze until the grass started to flicker and smoke.

Eventually the fire took hold and Slade removed his hat and started to fan the smoke down into the tunnel.

It wasn't long before the evil fumes reached the two frightened foxes who began coughing and spluttering, hardly able to breathe.

Slade heard the coughing and laughed out loud. Soon he'd have two more pelts to hang in his barn. It was just a question of time.

"Copper! Copper!" he called out to his dog, who stopped digging and waited as Slade came around to his hole. "We got him now for sure. This is their only way out."

Slade aimed his gun at the hole and waited, Copper ready to spring at his side.

They heard some movement from within the tunnel and Copper almost jumped forward, ready to attack.

"Steady, boy! Steady," said Slade, smiling at his dog's enthusiasm.

But no foxes appeared.

"Tod! We're trapped!" Vixey spluttered, turning her head from side to side, trying to find some air.

Tod looked toward the hole and could just about see Slade's hobnail boots and Copper's claws outside. So . . . they were both waiting at that end, were they?

Vixey slumped to the floor, her coughing getting worse all the time. They didn't have much longer now.

Tod prodded her gently to her feet and then helped her along the tunnel toward the smoke. At first she tried to resist, but then she seemed to get beyond caring and just went where Tod pushed her, her eyes big and streaming with tears.

Tod felt terrible that he had brought so much trouble into her life and even more terrible that now he was going to have to force her even further into the smoke. But he knew that, if they were to survive, there was only one way out of there and that was actually across the fire.

"This is our only chance," Tod gasped, as they neared the rear entrance.

They could hardly see any daylight at all through the hole, just gray and white smoke and orange flames. It was against all their instincts to do so, but the two foxes took as deep breaths as they could manage and plunged up and out through the furnace.

"Oh, no!" screamed Amos Slade, and his mouth dropped in amazement as his victims burst out and away. "Oh no . . . no! I just don't believe it!"

Copper did though, and without waiting for the instruction, leaped off to pursue the two fleeing foxes.

Refreshed by the cool, clean air in their lungs, Vixey and Tod seemed to fly away from Copper and quickly disappeared into the rocks and bushes.

Tod looked around at the countryside while he was running and, motioning to Vixey to follow, ran straight toward a steep escarpment. He knew that Copper and the Hunter would get

on their trail very soon, and across open country the bullets would have no trouble finding their mark.

Up and up they climbed; several times Vixey nearly fell and would have given up completely but for the terrifying sound of Copper barking not very far below them.

Soon the climbing got easier and then the land leveled out so that they found themselves on a small plateau.

Vixey collapsed and drew in long deep gulps of air. But Tod would not rest. He knew they had to find a way of losing Copper, who was still determinedly following the foxes up the cliff.

A little way along the plateau, Tod could hear the sound of running water. When he investigated he found that it was a waterfall which bubbled and frothed down to the valley below. Across the top of the waterfall a tree trunk had got caught among the rocks; suddenly Tod had an idea.

He raced back to Vixey and told her that they had to go on. She had just begun to think the very same thing as the scent of Copper was getting stronger all the time.

Tod led her along to the top of the waterfall. She looked puzzled, for there didn't seem to be anywhere to go from there.

Curiously, she waited as Tod told her to watch him carefully.

Jumping up a small tree, Tod ran along one of its branches which overhung the water and, pausing to check his balance, suddenly leaped from the branch onto the tree trunk which straddled the waterfall.

Luckily, the surrounding rocks were holding the trunk quite firmly, and Tod was able to walk along it to dry land without much difficulty. As soon as he landed he turned and motioned for Vixey to follow him.

Vixey looked dubiously from the branch down to the tree trunk. She'd never really been one for climbing or jumping but it looked as though she didn't have any choice.

Tod smiled and waved to her encouragingly.

So, gathering up all her courage, Vixey made her way toward the little tree and prepared to jump.

She found it surprisingly easy to get along the branch, but the sight of the flowing water beneath her almost made her lose her balance.

She looked over toward Tod, who was getting very anxious lest Copper should arrive on the scene.

Seeing his frightened glance toward the edge of the cliff, Vixey threw herself toward the tree trunk, and then raced along it and onto the shore.

Tod was very proud of her and intended to tell her so as soon as they had the time. Right then they had to get out of there so that Copper wouldn't see them and after a quick nuzzle, they were off running and dodging through the trees as fast as they could.

Poor Copper hadn't found it as easy to climb the cliff as the foxes. His claws weren't half as sharp and he had a lot more weight to carry.

When he eventually reached the plateau he too collapsed in a big furry heap, expecting to find his victims trapped before him. But, of course, they were nowhere to be seen.

Copper frowned. They had to be here. There was just nowhere for them to go, the plateau was surrounded by water.

He pulled himself to his feet and started to

sniff around. Their scents were very strong, so why couldn't he see them?

His nose lead him to the small tree from which they had made their escape. But suddenly his head jerked up as a new and rather . . . well . . . *frightening* smell assailed his nostrils.

He bent his bead and sniffed again. At that time Amos Slade arrived panting on the scene.

"Copper!" he called out.

But Copper was far too interested in his new discovery to pay any attention to Slade.

If only he could remember where he had smelled that scent before. He sniffed really hard, wondering why he felt so uneasy.

Slade just thought that the two foxes were hiding somewhere around the tree and started to aim his gun, ready to shoot when they emerged.

"We've trapped him now!" Slade called out happily to Copper.

But then his smile faded as a huge black shadow reared over the ground in front of him.

Slade turned, terrified, as the gigantic angry bear lashed out with his paws.

He swung his gun around and fired, too scared to take very good aim.

The shot ripped across the clearing and simply grazed the shoulder of the grizzly, who bellowed in rage and lunged forward to attack the pathetic human.

Slade backed off, not knowing that the edge of the cliff was directly behind him. Frantically he pulled another bullet from his pocket and loaded the gun with his shaking hands.

But just as he raised the gun to fire, the bear swiped the weapon completely out of his hands, knocking the Hunter way off his balance.

With a terrified scream, Slade fell backward and began to tumble down among the rocks and tufts of grass.

The big grizzly was so angry (and hungry) by now that he wasted no time in pursuing the rag-doll-like figure of Slade down the steep slope, grumbling and growling all the way.

Winded and frightened, Slade eventually came to a rolling stop at the bottom of the cliff. He sat up and shook his head to clear it of the ringing which went from ear to ear, but out of the corner of his eye he spotted the bear tumbling down after him.

Slade gave a little whimper and jumped to his feet, taking a couple of steps backward and keeping his eyes fixed on the snarling bear.

But as he walked his foot landed in one of his very own traps and Slade fell helplessly onto his back, waving his other leg in the air.

Desperately he pulled and yanked at the trap, but the iron was so heavy and so old that he needed some kind of leverage to get it open, and didn't stand a chance with just his bare hands, which were by now bleeding with the effort.

Slade looked from one side to the other for something to lever the trap open, and as he turned his head great beads of sweat were shaken off into the grass.

Just as the bear reached the level ground, Slade spotted Copper just behind him.

Valiantly, Copper leaped in between his master and the bear and growled ferociously.

The bear stopped, surprised more than anything that such a small animal should dare to challenge him. But his surprise soon disappeared and he lunged toward Copper, meaning to swat him out of the way with one of his huge paws.

But Copper was too quick for him, and dodged out of his way, still snapping and snarling to distract his attention.

The bear looked at Slade, as though wondering whether to bother with Copper at all, but the dog took his chance and threw himself onto the bear's neck and sunk his teeth in as far as he could.

The bear was absolutely livid and howled in anger. A huge paw came around and smacked Copper loose from his neck to land sprawling on the ground.

Copper rolled over back onto his feet and narrowly missed being flattened by the lunging

bear. He jumped again and reached the same target on the bear's neck as before, and felt the warm sickly taste of the bear's blood as his teeth sank even deeper than before.

This time Copper was determined to hang on . . . and hang on he did, despite the painful smack from one of the hefty paws. The bear attempted to swing the dog loose, but still he hung on, thinking that at last he was getting somewhere in this fight.

But the big grizzly knew more tricks than that, and rolled his huge body down onto the ground, smashing poor Copper under his head so that his teeth were almost knocked into the back of his throat.

Copper wriggled and kicked and bit any bear that came within an inch of his mouth, and eventually managed to free himself.

But now Copper had been severely winded, and knew that, unless something happened, the bear was bound to kill him.

As Copper threw himself at the bear's head, Slade looked around desperately as he struggled to remove the still tightly clenched trap. A glint of metal in the bushes suddenly caught his eye.

It was the gun! It had fallen there when the bear had swiped it from his hands, and now it was just a little way away, lying in the undergrowth.

With one look at the bloody fight still continuing, Slade dragged his painful leg toward the gun. Inch by inch, he crawled and scrambled, stretching out his hand, groping and clawing toward the weapon which could save his and Copper's lives.

Far away from the battleground, Tod and Vixey were getting higher and higher up the mountain. They were a little bit puzzled why they had not heard Copper's barking for some time, but just supposed that he was not as good at climbing as they were.

Tod noticed that the air was getting cooler and he would stop every so often to see if he could hear or see either one of their pursuers.

Suddenly an anguished cry echoed around the valley.

Vixey just kept on running, her curiosity completely outweighed by her fear. But Tod skidded to a halt and listened carefully.

From far down below he sensed, rather than heard, Copper's cries as the bear came nearer and nearer to triumph.

"Tod!" called out Vixey, realizing he wasn't following her and wondering why.

Tod looked from his mate to the valley below. Despite everything that Copper had done, Tod could not bear the thought that he might be killed. But then he didn't want to lead Vixey back into danger. Poor Tod just didn't know what to do.

Down below the foxes, Slade had still not succeeded in reaching his gun, and every time he looked at Copper, the brave dog seemed to be bloodier and bloodier.

The bear had sensed that his opponent was tiring and lashed out with his paws, leaving terrible scratch marks all over Copper's body.

Finally, Copper was beaten to the ground and, despite several attempts, found that his trembling legs just refused to carry his weight any longer.

The grizzly snarled. Now was the time for the kill. He pulled himself up to his gigantic full height and raised one of his front paws for the final blow.

Cooper closed his eyes and waited for death. But the blow was never to strike home. For just as the bear's paw began its downward strike, Tod threw himself at the animal's huge head and sunk his teeth into one of his ears, drawing a fountain of grizzly blood.

The bear bellowed with pain and anger, his head jerking backward in an attempt to shake off his attacker.

But Tod clung on grimly, his hind legs being thrown from side to side in mid-air.

Finally, he could hang on no longer and felt himself flying toward some nearby rocks. He rolled once, twice, and then quickly regained his footing, knowing that the bear would strike back, and that the only thing to do was to run and try to lead him away from Copper.

Tod scrambled up the hill, glancing over his shoulder to see the bear clumsily trying to follow him. But soon the fox came to a kind of rift in the ground. He tried to jump across to a ledge, but his judgment and energy had been severely damaged by the day's events and, missing the ledge completely, Tod tumbled down the slope toward the waiting bear.

The puzzled bear looked down as a heap of fox landed right between his legs. But Tod was too quick for him, and as a hairy paw lashed out for his eyes, Tod raced away again, the bear lumbering after him.

Tod was breathing heavily and noticed that he was following exactly the same path toward the waterfall that he and Vixey had taken earlier. Perhaps, he thought to himself, I can lose the bear exactly the same way that we lost old Copper.

But the bear knew the mountain much better than either Tod or Copper and, realizing the spot toward which Tod was running, he took a different path and arrived there at exactly the same time as the panting fox.

The two animals regarded each other for a

second. The bear snarled, showing an endless row of gleaming white teeth.

But Tod was unimpressed and, not even waiting for the bear to make the first move, he sprang up toward the teeth and bit their owner's cheek as hard as he could.

Thinking it very unwise to hang around near the mouth of the bear, Tod let go pretty quickly this time and jumped sideways to the ground as the grizzly's back foot came down to smash him flat.

Now the bear was on all fours and Tod took the opportunity to take a lump out of his neck— in the same place where Copper had struck home before.

The bear was really in pain now. He just couldn't believe that two such smaller animals would dare to attack him, let alone be able to hurt him, and he was beginning to feel dazed and confused.

He lashed out at Tod again, this time hitting him full in the face and sending him sprawling toward the log that spanned the top of the waterfall.

Tod landed half in the water and half on the log itself, and just managed to drag himself up out of the rushing torrent.

But the bear was wasting no time and already had one paw on the edge of the log, which was wobbling dangerously with his weight.

One step . . . two . . . and SNAP!

With just one paw left on dry land, the bear suddenly found that the trunk had snapped completely in two and his half was rushing toward the edge of the waterfall at an alarming rate.

At first Tod thought his troubles were over, but as the trunk split, his half rebounded into the side of the cliff and the jar sent Tod crashing into the water as well.

In his panic he grabbed the first thing that came in sight . . . which just happened to be the piece of trunk to which the bear was clinging as well.

The bear, seeing his hated opponent, forgot

all about the impending danger and started to inch along toward the soaking fox.

Tod just had time to feel the thwack of the bear's paw when the two of them found themselves falling down . . . down over the edge of the waterfall to the rocks below.

Both animals disappeared into the swirling waters and for a few seconds the surface was still.

Then Tod's head appeared, gasping and spluttering as the water gushed into his eyes, his ears and his mouth. Struggling wildly, he managed to claw his way to the bank where, exhausted and terrified, he collapsed onto the pebbly sand.

Tod closed his eyes in pain as his flooded lungs tried to empty themselves of stream water. He gagged and left a little pool of water in front of him, when he moved to a drier spot.

A sixth sense suddenly told him that he was not alone any more and he raised his head, not particularly caring whether it was the bear or not.

It was Copper, who breathed a sigh of relief at finding Tod still alive.

The dog approached warily. He had so many things he wanted to say to Tod, after all he owed him his life, but after everything that had happened he wasn't sure what to do or say.

The two animals stared at each other, not moving a muscle. But then the sound of a gun being cocked made both of them start and look around.

It was Amos Slade and he had his gun aimed directly at Tod!

Copper's eyes widened in horror and disbelief. Surely his master couldn't mean to kill Tod now, he *must* have seen how he had saved his life. He whimpered slightly as Slade's finger moved toward the trigger.

Tod rested his head wearily on his paws; he had no energy left for running or fighting, it was all over now.

But Copper was not finished yet. He limped toward Slade and placed himself directly in front of the gun, completely obstructing the Hunter's aim.

"C'mon, Copper," said Slade, waving a hand at the dog. "Get out of the way!"

But Copper stood his ground. Slade would have to kill him first if he wanted Tod so badly.

Slade looked down at his dog and then raised the gun threateningly and took aim once again, hoping that it would scare Copper out of the way.

But Copper sat very, very still, and stared up at Slade, pleading, begging, willing him to relent.

Slowly . . . very slowly . . . Slade lowered his gun and gave a little shrug of disbelief at what he had just witnessed.

"Well, c'mon then, boy. Let's go home," he

said softly, and turned his back on the clearing, not even sure that Copper would want to go home with him after what he had just seen.

Copper waited for a second or two and then started to limp after his master.

Tod shook his head and struggled to his feet, wanting to say goodbye. He was about to call out when Copper turned, but still neither of them had any real words to say to each other. So, just before Copper left the clearing Tod smiled, a warm, friendly smile which the dog returned instantly. And then he was gone, limping after the man who tried to teach him to hunt every living thing . . . but hadn't quite succeeded.

Chapter 7

Big Mama was awakened from her owly dreams by the familiar sound of pecking. She opened one eye and looked up sleepily to where Boomer was busily hammering away at the tree trunk while Dinky looked on.

When Boomer felt he had pecked enough, Dinky squeezed through his legs and peered into the resulting hole.

"Sssh! This is it. We got him for sure this time," said Dinky, motioning for Boomer to stop his giggling.

Inside the hole strange shapes and colors began to move, and the two birds could no longer make out the shape of the hairy little caterpillar they were trying to catch.

"Hey! What's going on?" cried Dinky, blinking as the colors grew brighter and brighter.

"Oh, my gosh!" exclaimed Boomer, almost falling off his branch in amazement.

Dinky shook his head and clung on to Boomer, hoping it was all a dream.

"Wh-what's happening!" Dinky kept on asking.

Suddenly a spectacularly colored vision burst out from the black hole in the tree. The two birds' eyes swam with reds and blues and yellows and oranges as the beautiful butterfly flapped its wings and fluttered around them.

"Hey! There's something very familiar about those eyes!" exclaimed Boomer, when suddenly the butterfly alighted right on his beak!

The butterfly batted its eyelids coyly at the surprised bird and jumped up and down a few times very cheekily. Somehow the butterfly seemed to be *displaying* himself to the birds, as though he wanted to show them something.

"Nah . . . it couldn't be!" said Dinky, gradually realizing just who the butterfly reminded him of too.

But it was! Yes, Squeeks the caterpillar had metamorphosed into one of the most beautiful butterflies ever, and now he wanted to show off his wonderful new colors to the two birds who had been trying to catch him for so long.

Squeeks decided that it was time to go, and fluttered down past Big Mama's hole.

"Bye, Squeeks," she called out, confirming the two birds' suspicions. "Bye . . . Good luck, honey!"

And the birds all watched as the stunning little creature disappeared into the forest.

"Ouch! You're killing me . . . Ow!" A rude voice broke into the peacefulness of the day and made the birds all turn toward the Widow's house.

It was Amos Slade who was having the bandage on his foot removed by the Widow.

Upon his return from the forest, he had thought that the least he could do was to let the Widow know that Tod was still alive and well. He had felt secretly guilty about what had happened, and the sight of Copper defending his friend to the last had mellowed even the Hunter's toughened old heart.

When the Widow had seen Slade's ripped and bleeding foot she had immediately ordered him into the house and proceeded to nurse him. She even quite enjoyed it, for since Tod had gone she had had nobody but herself to look after.

"Amos Slade, will you hold still. You're behaving like a child!" the Widow laughed, trying to keep the wriggling Slade still.

"Well, for gosh sakes! You're hurting my foot, woman!" Slade complained bitterly.

The Widow regarded Slade's unbandaged foot and gave it a soothing pat.

"Nonsense! Your foot's mending fine!" she told him, proud of her own handiwork.

Amos Slade grimaced, as though in the most

horrible pain, and cried out, hoping to evoke some sympathy as he was getting to like being nursed and mothered by the Widow.

"You'll soon be your old self," said the Widow, then laughed to herself, reflecting on what she had just said. "Oh, landsakes! I don't know if I like that!"

Slade crossed his arms and sulked; in truth even *he* didn't like his old self very much, but he wasn't going to admit such a thing to the Widow.

"Oh, do be careful! Oooh! Ow! Ouch!" cried out Slade, as the Widow put on a nice clean bandage again.

"Humph!" grunted Chief, his head sticking out of his barrel listening to the goings-on over at the Widow's house. "He's sure making a big fuss over a little hurt foot!"

Copper looked over at the old dog in disgust, remembering the groans and moans and carryings-on he had had to listen to when old Chief's leg was hurt. He grunted and decided to say nothing, he was far too sleepy to have an argument with Chief.

Copper laid his head on his paws and closed his eyes again, sliding back immediately into a twilight world of dreams and half remembered memories.

"Copper, you're my very best friend."

The hound-dog's eyes flickered slightly as the voice of Tod drifted into his mind.

"And you're mine, too, Tod," he heard himself as a young pup.

"And we'll always be friends forever, won't we?"

"Yes, forever."

Far away, on the top of the hill, Tod and Vixey looked down toward the buildings at the bottom of the valley. They couldn't actually see the two barrels that belonged to Chief and Copper, but Tod knew they were there.

Like Copper, he too was remembering their promises from so long ago, and the words of

Big Mama when she had warned him that forever was a long time.

Tod smiled. Big Mama had been wrong. They *were* still friends, even though they would probably never meet again, and they would both always remember the days when they were young.

He turned to Vixey and nuzzled her gently. Now he had a new life and a new family of his own to look forward to, and he hoped that Copper would always be just as happy as he felt right there and then.

A Dog in a Million!

Pete's best friend is Mishmash—a big, friendly dog who thinks he's human. Mish sleeps in a bed, eats at the table, and takes bubble baths. He hops into cars hoping for rides, adopts an imaginary playmate, and even gives a party for his dog friends! Join Pete and Mishmash as they get mixed up in one hilarious adventure after another.

The MISHMASH books, by Molly Cone
illustrated by Leonard Shortall:

_____	56083	$1.50	MISHMASH
_____	43711	$1.75	MISHMASH AND THE SUBSTITUTE TEACHER
_____	43135	$1.75	MISHMASH AND THE SAUERKRAUT MYSTERY
_____	43682	$1.75	MISHMASH AND UNCLE LOOEY
_____	29936	$1.50	MISHMASH AND THE VENUS FLYTRAP

If your bookseller does not have the titles you want, you may order them by sending the retail price (plus 50¢ postage and handling—New York State and New York City residents please add appropriate sales tax) to: POCKET BOOKS, Dept. AMM, 1230 Avenue of the Americas, New York, N.Y. 10020. Send check or money order—no cash or C.O.D.s and be sure to include your name and address. Allow six weeks for delivery.

133

There's No Stopping

Danny Dunn!

Danny Dunn, science fiction hero, with his friends, Irene and Joe, can't stay away from mystery and adventure. They have shrunk to the size of insects, traveled back in time, sunk to the ocean floor, and rocketed through outer space!

**The DANNY DUNN books,
by Jay Williams and Raymond Abrashkin:**

____	44383	$1.95	DANNY DUNN AND THE SMALLIFYING MACHINE #1
____	56092	$1.75	DANNY DUNN, INVISIBLE BOY #2
____	44382	$1.95	DANNY DUNN, SCIENTIFIC DETECTIVE #3
____	43877	$1.95	DANNY DUNN AND THE UNIVERSAL GLUE #4
____	44340	$1.95	DANNY DUNN AND THE HOMEWORK MACHINE #5
____	43404	$1.95	DANNY DUNN AND THE SWAMP MONSTER #6
____	43678	$1.95	DANNY DUNN AND THE ANTI-GRAVITY PAINT #7
____	43680	$1.95	DANNY DUNN, TIME TRAVELER #8
____	43679	$1.95	DANNY DUNN ON THE OCEAN FLOOR #9
____	43681	$1.95	DANNY DUNN AND THE WEATHER MACHINE #10
____	43290	$1.95	DANNY DUNN AND THE FOSSIL CAVE #11
____	42684	$1.95	DANNY DUNN AND THE VOICE FROM SPACE #12
____	29977	$1.75	DANNY DUNN AND THE AUTOMATIG HOUSE #13
____	44381	$1.95	DANNY DUNN AND THE HEAT RAY #14
____	29976	$1.75	DANNY DUNN ON A DESERT ISLAND #15

ARCHWAY PAPERBACKS from Pocket Books